TO TRUST A STRANGER

When Sara Dent's landlord relinquishes his business interests to his great-nephew Matt Harding, Sara fears that she will lose control of her struggling craft shop. And what — or who — is causing the strange noises in the empty rooms above? As she becomes reluctantly attracted to Matt, she discovers that her sleepy market town conceals sinister secrets. Sara must undergo emotional upheaval and life-threatening danger before her true enemies are revealed, and she learns who can be trusted — and loved.

Books by Anne Hewland
in the Linford Romance Library:

STOLEN SECRET

ANNE HEWLAND

TO TRUST A STRANGER

Complete and Unabridged

LINFORD
Leicester

First published in Great Britain in 2006

First Linford Edition
published 2007

British Library CIP Data

Hewland, Anne
    To trust a stranger.—Large print ed.—
Linford romance library
1. Love stories
2. Large type books
I. Title
823.9'2 [F]

ISBN 978–1–84617–757–6

Published by
F. A. Thorpe (Publishing)
Anstey, Leicestershire

Set by Words & Graphics Ltd.
Anstey, Leicestershire
Printed and bound in Great Britain by
T. J. International Ltd., Padstow, Cornwall

This book is printed on acid-free paper

1

One minute, Sara was sitting in the queue of traffic, wondering uneasily what she might find in her upper floor once she'd got hold of the key — and the next, the lights had changed and the four-wheel-drive vehicle in front of her jerked backwards. She felt the crunch as well as hearing it. Jamming her hand on to the horn, she glared at the sleek dark shape looming over her bonnet.

Just when she was in a hurry too. She fumbled for the door handle. It was only this afternoon that she'd finally decided what she was going to do, and having made the decision, she wanted to get on with it before she could change her mind. And now this idiot in front of her had backed into her car.

She scowled at the approaching driver, receiving an impression of someone tall, tanned and broad-shouldered in jeans and a black T-shirt as he joined her in looking down at the point of impact. A rueful and heart-wrenching grin that might have bowled her over if she hadn't been distracted. 'Hey, I'm sorry. I'm not used to driving on this side of the road. But it doesn't look too bad.'

Sara had to admit that it had sounded a lot worse than it was. The bumper must have taken most of the shock. But it was bad enough. 'My light's broken.' And the distinctive midnight-blue paint was scraped in several places. She pushed the bronze-gold curls behind her ears, ready for battle. If he thought he could charm his way out of his obligations on this, he could think again. 'We'll exchange details if you don't mind.'

The lights had changed again and other cars were edging round them as he was patting his pockets. 'Look, I'm not sure of the current procedure over here, but I'm in one hell of a rush, late for two places at once.' The search

2

successful, he was scribbling on a scrap of paper. 'Here. Get it seen to and bill me. Whenever you like.' Before she could object, the paper was thrust into her hand and he was slamming his door behind him.

'Hey, wait a minute,' Sara shouted. All she had was a mobile number and that was no guarantee of anything. 'How do I know you'll keep to this?'

He was leaning through the window as he moved off. 'It's OK. You can trust me.'

'I don't even know your name.' Her words were lost as he accelerated, taking the road towards the bypass. She squinted after him. She hadn't thought to take his vehicle number either. Too late now, but everything had happened so quickly. Follow him? By the time she had leapt back into her car and started up, the lights were changing again — even if he had been in sight. Which he wasn't.

She resisted the urge to rest her head on the steering wheel, but her hands were shaking — delayed reaction. And she was annoyed with herself. She knew exactly what Tony would have said — that's the last you'll see of him, you've been taken for a ride. Doubly annoying that she was even considering Tony's opinion. Tony was history and had been for over four years now.

She was an independent woman with her own business who had more pressing concerns than minor knocks to her car. If she had to pay for the repair herself, tough — she would deal with it.

But she couldn't prevent the gloomy thought that every penny counted at present and that she could ill afford even a small garage bill. At least the customised pink stripes down each side of her car had seemed OK. That would have cost a packet — and she'd had the blue and pink done specially to be the same as the painted signboard for the shop. A useful advert.

Never mind all that. Time to snap out of worrying about distracting encounters with good-looking strangers and get on. Though by now, investigating eerie noises in the attic was the very last thing she felt like doing.

Somewhere behind the sturdy front door, Sara could hear the doorbell jangling. She turned to stare out across the fields where the traffic was buzzing along the new bypass. Was the old man all right? It didn't usually take this long. She rang again, pressing harder this time and with panic rising in her chest. 'Mr Peasholm? Are you there?'

At last. Sara heard shuffling footsteps and the tapping of a stick. A frail voice called, 'I'm coming.' Phew. Poor Mr Peasholm. She wished she didn't have to trouble him like this, but there was no other way.

Now the door was catching on the mat as Mr Peasholm struggled to open it. Sara pushed as the old man pulled and his face lit up as he saw her. 'I got your message, my dear. I'm so glad you're here today. Come in, come in. now, you will stay for a cup of tea?'

Sara hesitated. 'Just for five minutes,'

she said cheerfully. 'I'm afraid I can't stop long. And I'll make the tea. I'm always happy to see you. You've been so good to me.'

She was so lucky to be three years into her dream of running a craft shop in the small northern market town of Beckthwaite — and even luckier to have Mr Peasholm as her landlord.

Not Mr Peasholm's fault that, after several bouts of illness, he could no longer play an active part in caring for his properties. He had always been on the ball if anything needed seeing to, summoning joiners and plumbers in the blink of an eye. All the more reason for Sara to help him out by sorting the present problem herself. And if she could just get hold of the key without worrying him too much . . .

Sara put the kettle on and followed him into the drawing-room, with its solid pre-war furniture. She cleared her throat uneasily. 'I was hoping to borrow the key to the upper floor?'

Mr Peasholm seemed to be concentrating on his feet, making little stuttering steps to reach his high-backed armchair. Even as he eased himself into the chintz-covered cushions, he avoided looking at her. 'You don't need to trouble yourself with anything up there. You have enough to do.'

'No trouble at all.' This was difficult. Sara didn't want to worry him too much. She shivered and hoped the old man hadn't noticed. 'The thing is — I think a bird might have got in.' Knowing as she spoke that no bird could possibly be responsible for the scraping, dragging sounds. 'If I could have a key permanently, I could help out up there with all kinds of things. Any problems with the roof, for instance.'

She sighed. How much better for Mr Peasholm if he had accepted her offer to buy the shop outright as she'd originally hoped. When she'd had the money. Out of the question now, with business not being too good.

Surprisingly he was smiling. 'There's something I've been meaning to tell you. I've found a solution — to all our problems.' He beamed up at her. Like a magician revealing a white rabbit. 'There's someone I want you to meet.'

Oh, dear. When all she wanted was to collect the key and dash off again. 'I'm really sorry, but I'm afraid I can't manage it today. If I could just collect the key . . . '

Mr Peasholm was ignoring her. 'My great-nephew will be arriving at any moment.'

'Nephew?' Sara tried to appear encouraging, but this was a complication she could do without. She frowned for a moment, mentally going through various relations Mr Peasholm had mentioned. None seemed to visit him much and indeed many of them seemed to be scattered around the globe. 'I thought your nephew was working in America?'

'That's right. But he's back in

8

England now. Has a few things to sort out and then he's going to settle here, with me.' Mr Peasholm's face was glowing with pride. 'And you'll be able to meet him at last.' He chuckled. 'I knew he would be back today, that's why I was so pleased when you phoned.'

'Um.' Sara's eyes flickered over to the photo on the mantelpiece. Yes, she had heard about Mr Peasholm's great-nephew, Matthew, and the way he was always dashing around the world, finalising deals or whatever he did. Mr Peasholm always seemed vague about it and hadn't even seen him since that branch of the family had emigrated, years before. But there he was in the photo, shaking someone's hand and receiving some prestigious award or other.

Sara bit her lips together. Oh, yes, she knew the type, didn't she? Only too well. That was why she and Tony had split up. And now the kettle was boiling, puffing clouds of steam across the kitchen and out into the hall. She hurried to see to it while Mr Peasholm raised his voice and carried on chatting but she couldn't concentrate on what he was saying.

Tony had been totally committed to a workaholic lifestyle and the first heady excitement of loving him had turned to misery and frustration. There had been hardly any time when Sara and Tony could be together. She had been so certain she would love him for ever but no, never again would she fall for somebody so arrogant, so self-centred, so . . . She carried the two mugs into the drawing-room.

'So you see, it really will be for the best,' Mr Peasholm was saying. 'Don't you think so?'

'Er — sorry?'

'That I'm going to hand all the responsibility over to Matthew. He's going to take charge of everything from now on.'

'Oh! That's great. Yes.' Sara tried to sound enthusiastic. There was no doubt that Mr Peasholm deserved a rest, but she had a horrible feeling that this great-nephew would walk all over him. Robbing him of the last of his independence. And another thought — what if he tried to walk all over his tenants too? As in me, Sara thought. Oh, no. No way. That just must not happen.

She gulped her tea down, luckily she'd put plenty of milk in hers, and looked at her watch. Still no sign of nephew Matthew, and she wasn't sorry. 'I'm afraid I really can't wait any longer. I need to get back before it gets dark.' She shuddered, remembering there was no electricity supply in the upper rooms. Why bother with this, a little voice in her head asked? Why not leave the noises to the redoubtable Great Nephew Matthew? For a moment she was tempted. But only for a moment.

No need to be giving Matthew the free run of her little sanctuary one minute sooner than absolutely necessary. The craft shop represented her dream and her independence, and she wanted to keep it that way. 'I'll look forward to meeting your nephew another time,' she assured him cheerfully.

Mr Peasholm nodded sadly. 'Something will have cropped up.'

Sarah sighed. Just the kind of thing Tony had always said, as he let her down yet again. She felt sorry for Mr P, waiting for this nephew with eager anticipation in his eyes. 'I'll still be able to pop round and see you, won't I?' she asked suddenly. She had always made a point of bringing the rent cheque round in person, but no doubt Matthew would be instigating some auto-debit banking system.

Mr Peasholm laughed. 'I certainly hope so.' He patted her arm. 'I have such fond memories of that shop and running it myself, in the early days. I won't need cheering up any more, once Matthew has lifted all my cares from my shoulders, so to speak, but I shall still welcome your visits.'

Sara smiled. 'That's great.' And perhaps everything would be fine and she mustn't begrudge Mr Peasholm's chance to lighten the burden of responsibility. Except that she had an uneasy feeling something didn't seem quite right.

Already however, the autumn sun-light was casting slanted shadows across the old man's lawn. She said gently, as Mr Peasholm made no move, 'You haven't given me the key yet.'

'Ah.' his eyes shifted warily. 'You're right. Time's marching and I'm prat-tling away.' Mr Peasholm heaved himself out of his chair and rooted in a drawer, panting a little. He swayed against the sideboard, eyes closed. 'Mr P? Are you all right?' Sara grasped his shoulders.

'Yes, of course. Just one of my silly spells.' Mr P was leaning against the sideboard but he seemed to have a healthy colour in his face. 'Quite gone now. I'm sorry, my dear, I don't seem to have the strength to look for the key.

But if you come again tomorrow, you'll be able to meet Matthew at the same time, won't you?'

In spite of her frustration, Sara couldn't help smiling. She wasn't quite sure that she believed in the funny turn. Mr P's sharp grasp of events was ensuring she was not to be let off the nephew-hook so lightly. She said, 'It would have to be later on. I left John next door keeping an eye out for my customers today, but I can't expect him to do it two days in a row — that wouldn't be fair.'

'John?' Mr Peasholm paled as he put a hand to his forehead. His voice was almost a whisper. 'I thought he'd retired by now. One of my other tenants told me he had.'

'Come and sit down. Are you feeling faint again? I can let myself out.' he certainly wasn't pretending this time. Sara was aware of how fast his heart was pounding in the thin chest. Should she wait a while? She didn't want to leave him like this.

She settled him into his leather armchair, talking gently to take his mind off his symptoms. 'You remember John? Well, of course you do. The jeweller next door. You've known him for years, haven't you? Yes, I'm sure he must be thinking of retiring soon and I shall miss him.'

It was working. Already Mr Peasholm was beginning to recover. 'He's been so helpful and obliging, right from day one. But it isn't fair to take his good nature for granted. And I'd do the same for him, but he's never asked. Just as well really as I don't know much about mending clocks or making valuations so I couldn't be much help there. I could sell the occasional diamond bracelet I suppose. That wouldn't be too difficult. Now, you sit there while I take the cups through.'

'Don't bother with the cups. They won't take me a moment.' The voice seemed much stronger now.

'No trouble,' Sara called over his shoulder. She was already in the kitchen and the few minutes it would take her to wash, dry and put everything away would give Mr P time to recover completely. Half-listening to any untoward noises from the sitting-room, she turned to the cutlery drawer too quickly and caught a large wooden jar labelled *Utensils*.

The jar tipped and everything slid over the kitchen surface. 'Clumsy,' she chided herself. Mr P's kitchen was always so neat. She began scooping up wooden spoons and tin openers — and stopped. Wedged in the bottom of the jar was a key, dulled and dusty through lack of use. Even without the creased cardboard luggage label attached with string, she knew at once what it was. *14a The Square*.

'So that's where it was,' she murmured. She dislodged it and took it out, turning to tell Mr P that they wouldn't need to turn the house upside down after all. From the sitting-room there came a crash of breaking glass. She hurried in to see Mr P staring down at the precious photograph. 'I wanted to show it to you,' he said mournfully. 'It's Matthew receiving his most recent award.'

She wanted to say, 'I could have got that down for you.' She bit the words back. Bad enough for Mr P that he couldn't manage to reach it without dropping it; the last thing he needed was having a young and agile person pointing this out to him. 'It's all right,' she said. 'We can easily get another frame for it.' She tidied the glass away and stopped in the act of putting the photo back on the mantelpiece. Was there something familiar about the smiling face in the smart city suit? No, the brief moment of recognition had gone.

And now she really would have to get back. In spite of his latest mishap, Mr P was looking more his normal self and she was certain he could safely be left. She hurried out to her beloved little Ford Fiesta, wincing at the sight of the front wing. She'd forgotten about that during the last half hour. One more problem she didn't have time for just now.

All the same, she hesitated as she unlocked the car door, still torn between her need to dash off and a feeling that she should do more here. She did so hope that Matthew would appreciate how much the old man needed kindness. A gentle approach. Yes, she would be ready to fight Mr P's corner for him whenever necessary.

She started the car and glanced at her watch. Not that coming dusk mattered now since she would be returning for the key tomorrow. At least she knew where it was. Or did she? She frowned. What had she done with it? Distracted by the picture frame incident, she couldn't remember. Unbidden, her right hand slid to her jacket pocket. Yes, it was there. She must have slipped it into her pocket without thinking.

She bit her lips as she moved off across the gravel towards the gateway.

Well, there was no point in taking it back when Mr P had intended giving it to her anyway. No, she would bring it back tomorrow. And she would be able to report that the problem upstairs, whatever it was, had been dealt with. That would impress Matthew, showing him what she was made of. There would be no need for him to be sniffing round her little domain on the pretext of sorting things out.

In the seconds while her concentration was diverted, a familiar four-wheel-drive vehicle swept on to the drive with a squeal of tyres. Missing her car by inches.

Not again. She didn't believe this. Not twice in one day. Sara braked and swerved, wincing at the sharp clunking noise as her mirror caught the gatepost. Simultaneously, her brain was putting everything together. No need to wonder who this was. Just the kind of vehicle, and the kind of driving, she would have expected.

No sign of the disarming grin now.

He was glaring at her as he jumped out, slamming his door shut. No doubt he was about to blame her when the fault was all his, sweeping in like that without looking. At least she would know where to get hold of him for the bill. That was a relief. But she had wasted quite enough time on him and had no intention of having her first meeting with her new landlord in this way. Not when she had the key in her pocket. She spotted a gap in the traffic and put her foot down.

He was standing in the gateway now, gazing after her. She couldn't resist it. She lowered the window and gave him a cheerful wave.

It was obvious who that had been, Matt thought grimly. And OK, he was having trouble manoeuvring his hired vehicle around and the knock by the lights had been his fault and these gateposts were narrower than he remembered, but she could have given him a chance to apologise.

He frowned up at the house.

Everything still looked OK, but where was Uncle Paul? Matt rang the bell several times and at last realised that the door wasn't locked and that his uncle was sitting in his chair, clutching a wooden container. He was shocked to realise how frail the old man looked, but managed to hide his feelings with an easy grin. 'Hi, Uncle. I got back as soon as I could. Told you it wouldn't take long.'

'I can't see the key. It's gone.' The old man shook the jar, which was obviously empty.

'OK.' Matt was speaking slowly and calmly. 'Which key do you mean? I have another set of house keys here, which you gave me last week, remember? When I first arrived. And I also have that big tin full of duplicates for all your properties. So we can sort something out. No need to worry.'

'You don't understand. Sara may have taken it. Go after her, Matthew. She thinks she's heard a bird but it's all a mistake. There's nothing up there. Nothing.'

'OK,' Matt said again. He was smiling reassuringly, but he was deeply concerned. From the start, he'd been in favour of allowing Uncle Paul to hang on to his independence for as long as possible, but now it seemed that the rest of the family had been right. Matt should have stepped in sooner. Uncle Paul was evidently very confused. His responsibilities were getting to be too much for him.

'The rooms above the shop have to stay locked. You'll get after her, Matthew, won't you? You must stop her.'

Matt stood up. 'Of course. I'll go right away.'

'I wanted to introduce you properly,' his uncle said, dolefully. 'I had it all planned. She's a lovely girl, a breath of fresh air. This has all been a misunderstanding.'

'Right.' Matt was striding over to the door. 'Don't worry,' he called over his shoulder. 'That's why I'm here. To solve all your problems.' Inside, he was fuming. Lovely girl? A breath of fresh air? So why was she stealing Uncle Paul's keys and upsetting him this way?

This was only reinforcing the family's opinions of her as one of those women who saw elderly men as easy prey. Appearing to be helpful, and making herself indispensable while she was only out for what she could get.

No, Matt thought grimly, he hadn't come over one moment too soon.

2

Since the opening of the bypass, Sara had a choice of two routes back into Beckthwaite. She chose the new road, which would be slightly longer, but also faster. If there wasn't a queue to get off.

Naturally, there was. What could be causing the hold up? She tapped her fingers on the steering wheel. As they crawled past the piece of tarmac that ended abruptly and which would eventually become a farther five miles of road when the next stage was completed, she saw a police car and several figures in jeans and anoraks, waving placards. Protesters. She'd forgotten about them.

They'd been interviewed in the local press, determined to protect an ancient area of woodland. Sara felt a certain sympathy with them because the woodland was beautiful and irreplace-able. Surely it would make sense to wait and see how well the first stage of the bypass was working before thinking about extending it? In fact, if she wasn't mistaken those other vehicles looked to belong to a TV news crew. She recognised the logos on the sides.

But at the moment, the protesters weren't actually in the woodland. She peered beyond the fence to a mass of makeshift tents and awnings. No, they were camping at the bottom of Helen's garden. Oh, no. Sara's heart sank.

Helen Allenwick had been a close friend of Sara's mother and there had always been a kind welcome for the small Sara in the large house and grounds. And now she was a reliable supplier of craftwork for Sara's shop.

How on earth would the nervous and retiring Helen be reacting to this intrusion? The queue was now at a complete standstill. Without thinking twice, Sara reached for her mobile phone.

'Hello? Yes?' Helen's voice sounded strained.

'Helen, it's Sara. I was just ringing to ask — are you all right?'

'Yes, I'm fine.' Helen's voice cracked. 'Oh, Sara, I don't know. There are all these people in my shrubbery. I don't know what to do.'

'I'm sure there's nothing to worry about. I'm on the bypass and the police are here. Can you see the blue lights?'

'No, not from here. Oh, thank you, Sara. That's a relief I must say.' Helen's voice was still quivering. 'I thought you were phoning about the embroideries. I've almost finished this batch. I don't suppose you'd like to pop in and collect what I've done, would you?'

It was obvious that Helen was in need of friendly contact. 'No problem,' Sara said warmly. Don't even think about how the sun would already be sinking behind the bank and the post office across the square and plunging her upper windows into gloom. 'I'll be with you in five minutes. As soon as we get moving.'

Helen greeted her with a relieved smile. Sara knew she had made the right decision. Quickly she reassured Helen about what was happening. 'Everything seemed fairly good-natured and they didn't look to be doing any damage.'

'You don't think they'll come up to the house, do you?' Helen's face drooped with worry. She shivered and pulled her thin beige cardigan round her shoulders.

'Goodness, no. It's the woods they're interested in. Look, come and sit down.' Sara ushered Helen to a chair, not feeling that her words were doing much good. This was the second time she was doling out tea and comfort in as many hours.

As Helen sipped her tea, clutching her cup in both hands to absorb the heat, she too was beginning to recover. 'I have a bag of work all ready for you — and there are a few more that just need finishing touches, to get them ready for hanging. As soon as I've finished this, I'll get on with them and I can drop them off at the shop tomorrow?' Unsure of herself, Helen always managed to turn a statement into a question.

'There's no hurry. Whenever you're ready.' Sara hesitated. Somehow Helen's reaction to all this seemed over the top. She had seemed very relieved to hear about the police presence and yet Sara felt there must be something more. 'Is there something else worrying you?' she asked cautiously. 'Please tell me if there is. I may be able to help.'

She was expecting the older woman to deny it, but Helen put her hands to her face. 'Oh, Sara. I don't know what I'm going to do. I should have seen this coming I suppose, ever since my brother, Bob, died and I discovered we had never been financially secure.'

Sara stared at her. 'I'm so sorry, I had no idea. You seemed to be coping so well after your brother died.'

'I've been doing my best, but I can't afford to live here any longer. I have to sell up. Urgently.'

'Oh, Helen. You'll have to lose this house? Is there no other way?'

'No, I'm resigned to that now.' Helen took a long calming breath and straightened her shoulders. 'It's far too big for me and I've been planning this for a while. But I just wish I'd got on with it sooner, because who's going to make any kind of offer now, with all those protesters at the bottom of my garden?'

'Perhaps they won't be there too long.' Sara's voice didn't sound convincing, even to herself.

Helen sighed. 'I've read the papers and seen what's happened to other sites. This kind of thing can go on for months, years even. If they decided to build tree houses or tunnels, there'll be no shifting them. But even so and if I could sell up tomorrow, it wouldn't be quite enough. Not after the financial mess Bob left. No.'

She sat up, straightening her shoulders and putting her cup down. 'I've decided. Seeing you has helped me to come to a decision. Something else I could have done a long time ago. Wait there a moment. I want to show you something.'

She got up, unlocked a small oak bureau and brought out a black metal cash box. Sara recognised the small red leather case inside and smiled. 'The Allenwick Star!'

Helen smiled. 'You remember.'

'Of course. As a child, it fascinated me. When you used to get it out and let me hold it if I'd been well behaved, that was a great treat.'

She spoke softly as Helen gently placed it within her outstretched hand. Almost thinking that if she spoke too loudly the star would dissolve. How many hours of work must have gone into producing this delicate piece of jewellery?

It was the emeralds that formed the star shape although Sara had always thought that the star points were more like petals, forming a diamond and emerald flower. A fairy flower, she had told herself as a child.

'I don't usually keep it in the house now. It's been in the bank for years, since before Bob died and that seems such a waste? What's the point of owning something like this if I can't appreciate it? It isn't as if there are any family members left who would expect to inherit.' Helen was speaking briskly. 'So that's it. I've made my decision.'

Sara blinked in surprise. 'You're not going to sell it?'

'Yes. My mind is made up. I have no choice, whichever way you look at it. I can't afford the insurance now. And I have to be practical. I must think of the pleasure it will bring to the purchaser — as well as being a life-saver for me.

'You have no idea, Sara, how I long to have the freedom to buy a small manageable bungalow. No more money worries, and even before those young people descended on me, this house was becoming a burden. No, they are the final straw and I shan't be sorry to go.'

Sara was shaking her head. This all seemed so sudden. But obviously Helen had been thinking about taking these two fundamental steps for some time. Even talking about them was making her seem more cheerful. Sara looked round the large, dimly-lit room seeing it with new eyes. Being such a frequent visitor, she hadn't noticed how shabby the once luxurious carpets and curtains had become.

'I'm going to get some valuations,' Helen said. 'Perhaps you can advise me?'

'Me? Well, if I can of course,' Sara said carefully. 'But perhaps your solicitor might be a more suitable person?'

Helen raised her eyebrows. 'He means well and is scrupulously honest. But he was Bob's solicitor too for all those years and I really don't feel that I want to rely on his advice. How about that jeweller's next door to your shop?

What's the name?'

'Oh, certainly,' Sara said with enthusiasm. 'Fletcher. John Fletcher. I can thoroughly recommend him. He's very knowledgeable, and he was helpful in selling some bits and pieces for me when Mum died. He'll get the best price possible for you.'

'I thought I should probably get more than one valuation.'

'Of course. And John will be able to suggest other reliable jewellers. He's very generous in that way.'

'Good.' Helen was gradually losing that white, strained look.

It seemed a shame in many ways, but Sara knew that trying to talk her friend out of her planned course of action would not have been at all helpful. And now that Helen was looking so much better, she knew that she must be off. 'If you're sure you'll be OK, I'd better go.'

'By all means,' Helen said. 'Silly of me to get so upset, but talking to you has really helped. Your mother used to be just the same, didn't she? I can get on with finishing the rest of my little hangings and cushions with a quiet mind now — I'll bring those in tomorrow.'

She was still eager, however, for Sara to take the large bag that was waiting in the hall. Perhaps every penny counted and as soon as possible, Sara thought. Well, she could help in a small way. She would give Helen's work the best possible chance of selling quickly and getting good prices by moving Celia's things and placing Helen's work in the centre of the window.

She knew Celia wouldn't like it, but that was just too bad. Funny wasn't it, that a brother and sister could be so different? Celia, with her constant demands and complaints was nothing like John and it was only occasionally that Sara succeeded in selling anything of hers.

In fact it was only for John's sake that she had ever agreed to display them. She did her best to tolerate Celia's moods and tried to be friendly to her, but it was far from easy.

Talking to Helen had shunted Sara's own problems to the back of her mind, but by the time she arrived at the shop, it was almost dark. There were dim standby lights showing in most of the premises around the square and Sara knew the buildings would be empty.

The market-square seemed so sleepy and picturesque during the day with its central area of original cobbles and the grey stone and slate of the upper storeys but now, it had a sinister feel.

She would need her torch, although at least the light in the shop would shine through to the stairs in the narrow hallway. Just as well. Since she never went upstairs, she used the treads as an impromptu storage space and they were covered with boxes and bags.

If only she'd had more time before rushing out this afternoon, she would have pushed them to one side, to make a way through. But a couple of customers had come in unexpectedly

— not that they'd bought anything.

And here was the torch exactly where she had thought it would be. Good. Wasn't it? That meant there was no possible reason to put things off. She realised suddenly that she might have welcomed the excuse. Her heart was thudding already. Batteries? Yes, all present and correct. A beam of light shone across the staircase.

That was odd. She must have shifted the boxes and bin bags after all. Strange that she didn't remember doing it. But never mind that. A good thing that she didn't need to waste any more time.

Anyway, she didn't need the shop light now. She switched it off. Some instinct was telling her to conceal her presence as far as possible. It would depend, wouldn't it, on what she found up there? No, don't think about that. She would be talking herself out of this in a minute. Get on with it.

Grasping the key in her right hand and the torch in her left, she mounted the stairs quickly, before she could change her mind. Would it be better to be very quiet, hoping to catch whatever it was unawares? Or loud, to frighten it off? She seemed to be going for quiet, but she wasn't sure she actually wanted to catch anything. Just to have a simple look and beat a swift retreat, having targeted the problem.

Inside, something moved. As if something — or someone even — had bumped into something else. Too big for a mouse. Sara froze, holding her breath. Sweat trickled between her shoulder blades. She couldn't hear anything now. Whatever it was must be listening too.

No, this was ridiculous. She had known all along that something was happening up here and the whole point was to find out. It couldn't possibly be another person when she had the key. Probably nothing more than timbers settling which often happened here in the evenings as the air cooled. A quick check would prove the rooms were empty and set her mind at rest.

She took a long overdue breath, turned the key, grasped the handle and pushed. 'There!' she said loudly. Because of course, the first room was empty. It looked exactly the same as when Mr Peasholm had first shown her round, three years ago. Three small dusty rooms with peeling pink and brown speckled wallpaper. Living accommodation for the shop, Mr P had told her. She remembered how she had been suddenly tempted. 'Could I live here, do you think? It wouldn't take much doing up.'

Mr P had been shaking his head. 'Not practicable I'm afraid. Appearances are deceptive — would cost far too much to make it safe. I wouldn't like to feel responsible. In case of any accident, you know.'

These rooms weren't as gloomy as she'd expected, however. She'd forgotten about the streetlights outside. She hardly needed the torch, but it would be useful for searching in corners because now she was here, she might as well look properly. She had no intention of making a return visit.

And into the second room — yes, everything fine.

But as she approached the last door, her heart was thudding. Something must have been making those noises. Something large. She closed her eyes as she grasped the handle — though heaven knew what good that would do. She snapped her eyes open again. Far better to see whatever might be lying in wait.

She pushed the door so wildly as she flung herself through that it swung shut behind her. There. Nothing.

'What did I tell you?' she said briskly, feeling braver now. There was only the grubby little kitchen area leading off this room and the kitchen door was standing open already. And she should check inside the cupboards too she supposed. Hang on, that was funny. She bent down and peered at the dust on the floorboards.

Behind her came the sound of

breaking glass. She whipped round, knowing that it had come from the room she'd just left. As if someone had dislodged one of the old jam jars. Her thoughts spiralled wildly.

Perhaps she herself had set the old boards and walls groaning as she'd crossed the room. And the vibrations had affected the shelf. Unlikely, however much she wanted to believe it.

Keep calm. She couldn't just stand here, shivering like a frightened rabbit. Somehow she had to get out of here. Do something decisive. But before she had worked out what the something decisive was going to be, she heard her own voice saying, 'I know you're in there. You'd better come out.' It sounded firm and strong. Odd when the rest of her was feeling so wobbly.

You're a fool, Sara Dent, but she was careful not to say that out loud. And what a fool she must seem, talking to an empty room and broken jar. Go and look. Get it over with and get on with the rest of the evening. Easier said than done. Her legs didn't want to move. Make them. One step, two — and the door was beginning to open.

She put a hand over her mouth, pushing the rising scream back down into her throat. The gap in the doorway widened. The torch, she thought suddenly and directed the beam at the opening.

A tall dark-haired figure was caught in the light. 'It's OK. Nothing to worry about.'

Sara stared at him, recognising Matthew Harding's strong features and broad shoulders only too well and twice over. Just like his photographs, she thought foolishly, swaying as the blood rushed back to her limbs. Should have realised why he seemed familiar. 'You idiot. What on earth are you doing? And how did you get in?'

'I have duplicate keys to all my uncle's properties. And I would very much like to know how you got in.'

Sara hesitated. 'I went to get the key from Mr Peasholm this afternoon.'

The grey eyes were cold now. 'And he gave it to you?'

'Well, not exactly.' Sara had to be scrupulously honest. 'He wanted to give it to me. He looked for it and then I found it in the kitchen. Mr Peasholm dropped something and I realised later I'd slipped the key into my pocket. When I ran to help him.' She flushed, knowing this sounded lame. No wonder great-nephew Matthew was looking so sceptical. She said hurriedly. 'No doubt you don't believe a word of it. But I can assure you that's what happened.'

Suddenly the frown disappeared and it was as if the sun had come out. His face altered completely. Sarah bit her lips to prevent a gasp. This man could have given Tony lessons in charm.

'I think we've got off on the wrong foot.' He extended a hand. 'We're forgetting the formalities, aren't we? Let's put that right. Matt Harding.'

Sara wasn't quite ready to forget the fright he'd given her. She managed a frosty smile. Matt's grip was warm and strong without being overpowering. A pity, an unwanted whisper in her head told her, that he was just another out-for-everything-he-could-get-at-the-expense-of-everyone-else kind of person. Because in more favourable circumstances she might have been attracted to him.

'Sara Dent,' she said. 'And you haven't answered my question. Why are you here? Oh, of course. Mr P told you what I was going to do.' She clicked her tongue in annoyance. Should have thought of that. 'I'm sure a bird has got in. Or something.'

'I didn't intend to startle you. Or to get here first.'

No, she supposed he wouldn't have. Was this meant to be an apology? 'Um,' she said, half beginning to think she might forgive him.

'I assumed you were up here already — and I know about the lights. But there was no need for you to tackle this. It's part of my duties as landlord.'

'You could hardly tackle everything at once,' Sara said. 'I was saving you a job.' Now that the mingled shock and relief were oozing away, she felt that she wasn't too sure about him. After that first smile, to put her at her ease, she supposed, there had been no sign of another. Almost as if he didn't trust her.

Now there was a note of exasperation in his voice. 'No, I'm taking over my uncle's affairs full time from now on. There are no short cuts. I want to discover everything for myself. Everything that's been going on.'

'Going on?' Sara stared at him blankly.

'I'm concerned about my uncle's interests.' He stared back.

'Well, of course you are.' Here we go. Here's where poor Mr P gets trampled on. Sara glared at him.

He glared back, gesturing around the empty rooms. 'I'm concerned about this, shall we say, wasted-space. Haven't discussed it with my uncle yet, but I'm sure this flat could be doing something far more useful. Space is money, you know.'

Just the kind of thing Tony would have said. And her money, no doubt. And she had even been on the brink of half-liking him. Just showed how deceptive a smile could be. 'What did you have in mind?' she asked coldly. As if she couldn't guess.

He didn't seem to notice the frost in her voice. 'You've hardly any storage space downstairs for a start. And if you're having to make use of the stairway . . . '

'So this is an excuse to put my rent up?'

'Not necessarily. But that's something I'll have to look at with all my uncle's properties. It wouldn't be fair to pretend otherwise. He has to make a living after all.'

Sara took a breath. 'Well, I'm fine thanks. I like my shop just as it is. And I'm perfectly willing to clear the stairs if you want to rent this out to someone else. But if you're looking to increase my payments, I'm afraid it's not on. I can't do it.'

He paused, putting both hands up in a gesture of appeasement. 'Go easy. We don't need to talk about money at this stage.'

Not at any stage, Sara thought bleakly. If the rent increased, she couldn't afford to stay. Simple as that. Oh, why did he have to come here, disrupting everything? 'Besides,' she said crossly, 'why were you messing about upsetting the jam jars? You'll be one short now. That will be a gap in your inventory. If you'd called out and made your presence known to me in the first place, you could have avoided that.'

He laughed, yet again taking Sara by surprise with the warmth that flashed across his face. 'An impulse — and not a sensible one. I got delayed on the bypass so at first I thought you would've been and gone. When you arrived and I realised you were behind me instead of ahead of me, I thought I'd scare you to death.

'So because I thought you'd have a

quick glance round and leave, I moved into each room as you left it. I know, I should have said something straight-away, but it would have worked, if it hadn't been for those jars. And I'm sorry because now I have scared you and it's got us off on the wrong footing. I didn't intend to, believe me.'

'Not at all,' Sara said. 'I don't scare easily, Mr Harding.'

Behind her there was sudden patter-ing of feet as a dark shape hurtled through the room. Instinctively, Sara leapt towards Matt and at once wished she hadn't as two strong arms shot out to catch her. She jolted away again in horror at herself. Whatever must he be thinking? But at least by the expression on his face, he seemed as startled as she was.

'Only a cat,' she said loudly. Already a cat was making for the kitchen skylight and a broken pane that Sara hadn't noticed. With a whisk of black tail it was through and away.

'So that explains it,' Matt said. 'I'll

see to that for you. Either myself or I'll get someone round. And they should be able to do it by accessing the roof so they won't need to trouble you. All solved. Very satisfactory.'

'Right,' Sara said, feeling she'd had enough excitement for one night and not resisting as Matt politely ushered her towards the outer door. This would be an ideal time, she supposed, watching him lock up, to offer to return Mr Peasholm's key. But she said nothing. Fortunately, Matt seemed to have forgotten about it. And she wasn't going to remind him.

Thoughtfully, she watched him walking across the square. Why park right over there — unless he hadn't wanted her to notice his arrival? A convincing story, she thought, but not quite convincing enough. And there was something about the way he looked at her, you would almost think he was wary of her for some reason.

Well, she was going to be wary of him too. She had every intention of keeping an eye on those rooms. She was convinced that the noises she'd been hearing had not been made by any cat. And the marks in the dust backed that up. Marks as if something heavy and bulky had been dragged along the floor.

And it seemed quite possible that great-nephew Matt knew a lot more than he was saying. All that stuff about storage and putting the rent up might well have been some kind of smoke-screen, distracting her from what was really going on up there. Oh, yes, she was definitely going to make use of the key to investigate further. On her own.

3

Less than a mile down the road, Matt pulled in. he wanted time to think, before he got back to his uncle's house. He didn't know what to make of that girl but he was more certain than ever that something was going on. Uncle Paul was so obviously worried about something.

Did it have something to do with Sara Dent and the supposed *noises*? He'd done his best, in spite of his suspicions, to be pleasant and friendly, but had come up against a shield she had cleverly erected around herself. Once or twice there had been moments when he'd felt she was on the brink of opening up, but no, whatever she was up to had prevented anything like that.

He had been waiting for her to offer to return the key and she hadn't taken the opportunity. Why should she want it? That seemed to prove his suspicions. He felt a twinge of regret that this vibrant, elfin girl with autumn-glow hair should be at the root of anything suspect. No, don't go there. Just thank your lucky stars that whatever she'd been intending up there, he'd put a stop to it for the moment. And he would get to the bottom of it, for Uncle Paul's sake if nothing else.

Sara looked round the shop, wishing it wasn't way too late to open up, even for half-an-hour. She didn't have a great deal of square footage, but took satisfaction in knowing she had used every inch to the maximum potential. The end wall, in the natural grey stone, held the paintings and embroidered hangings while two walls had pine shelving stuffed with pottery, carvings and candles.

Sara sighed. She needed light and bustle and lots of customers. She didn't want to be on her own. But the only people in sight were the group of youths who had taken to hanging around the clock tower. They seemed harmless enough, but John would occasionally go out and confront them. Of course, a jeweller had far more reason to be edgy than she had, but she did wish he wouldn't. It only antagonised them.

She jumped as the phone rang. Staring at it almost in panic because why was it ringing after dark? Who knew she was here? 'Oh, hello, John.' A feeling of warm relief. Of course she wasn't on her own. Not with John's shop through the adjoining wall.

'Sara? Is that you?' He sounded as surprised as she was. 'I didn't see a light.'

'I was just going.'

'I was ringing to see if everything was all right. I thought I saw someone letting themselves in a while ago — obviously with a key. But I couldn't see your car. I'd have done something sooner, but I've been busy. With a late customer.'

'Nothing to worry about,' Sara said,

knowing that she was sounding over hearty. 'My landlord's nephew, that's all.' she explained briefly that Matt would be taking over. 'I'm sure it will be for the best.'

'For the best. Yes.' John's voice had a faraway quality. 'I didn't know.'

Sara shook the handset. 'Not a good line. It's reassuring to know you spotted him coming in, you're very vigilant. I feel completely safe, knowing you're watching out — and particularly with those boys being out there.'

'They're not here again are they? I had a word only this afternoon and told them to move on.'

'No, it really doesn't matter,' Sarah said hastily, wishing she hadn't mentioned them. 'They're not doing anything. They're nowhere near the shops or the parked cars. And I'm going now. I won't get any more customers at this hour.' She thanked him again, remembering as she put the phone down that she'd intended rearranging the window.

Too late for that now, but at least she

could move Celia's things in readiness — perhaps putting a couple of eye-catching items of Helen's in the window and arranging it properly tomorrow. No need for anything more. If any tourists should be contemplating an evening stroll, those young men would put them right off. The boys might be harmless but they tended to be noisy.

It was an unsettling day all round and she just wanted to go home. She removed Celia's colourful items briskly. She didn't feel that the mystery of the noises had been solved at all. If only Matt hadn't insisted on butting in, she thought crossly.

Admit it, he had been unsettling in his own way and nothing to do with noises or cats. He gave an impression of sun and the outdoors somehow. Nothing at all like Tony whose tan had been fake and his fair hair gelled to perfection. There was genuineness about Matt — and that smile.

Forget it. No doubt he knew exactly

how and when to use the smile. He would be used to women falling at his feet and was using the same charm techniques with poor Mr Peasholm — and he might be related to him, but they hadn't met for years so it wasn't as if Mr P knew him well. Or could even be certain of being able to rely on him.

Well, Matt Harding needn't think the charm offensive would work with her. Even if she was in any way ready for another relationship, Matt Harding was the very last person she would consider.

There, that would do. A sudden movement in the square caught her attention, accompanied by shouts and laughter. She recognised the rounded shoulders and greying hair; oh, no — John had ignored her advice and had gone out to tackle the youths again on his own.

Now he was tapping their white van, which was pulled across several parking spaces. As she watched, wondering what to do, one of the youths pushed John and he staggered back a few feet.

She heard the crash as he bumped against the van's door panel.

Without thinking, Sara shot out, waving her mobile phone in one hand. 'Hey,' she called. 'Stop that. I've phoned the police.'

The youths froze. The ring-leader, the one who had pushed John and whose face was partly obscured by a black baseball cap, seemed to be glowering at her. The others were grinning but that was hardly reassuring. 'That won't do you no good,' one of them shouted.

John was brushing paint flecks from his shoulders, his face flustered. 'No, it's all right, Sara. I've had a word. These gentlemen were just leaving.' His announcement was met with a chorus of jeers and catcalls, but miraculously they were piling into the van and seemed to be obeying him. The van swung round, narrowly missing John's feet, and roared out of the square, choosing the wrong direction along the one way street by the baker's.

Sara relaxed. 'I don't know how you did that, but well done. Are you OK?'

John was still looking worried. 'So there's no need for the police to come out now. We'll have to phone again and put them off.'

'It's all right, I didn't ring them. I didn't have time. That was a bluff. But seriously, don't you think we should? Perhaps they could arrange to have more of a presence in the square.'

John laughed uneasily. 'I very much doubt whether the police would consider that justified. After all, the lads aren't really causing any trouble.'

Sara stared at him. 'One pushed you, John. I'm a witness. Isn't that an assault?'

'What? Oh, no. Nothing like that. He didn't actually touch me. I stepped back, not realising I was so near to the van. By the way, what was it you were telling me about your landlord? On the phone?'

Brave of John to be making light of it, but he still looked shaken. Sara was glad to go along with the change of subject, telling him more fully about Matt's take-over. Besides, John had upper rooms too — he might have heard the various species of livestock himself. And John would have been a better companion up there than the supercritical Matt. She wished she'd thought of that earlier.

As a distraction, this didn't seem to be working too well. She tried to emphasise the clash between herself and Matt, turning the whole episode into an amusing story as they walked back to John's door. 'I think I convinced him it was the cat, so I'm hoping he won't be sniffing round again. Matt, I mean — Mr P's nephew. Not the cat.' She laughed but John wasn't joining in. was he even listening? 'Are you all right?'

'Yes. Fine.' He put a hand to his forehead.

'I really think you should sit down. It must be delayed shock. You won't be staying any longer tonight, will you? I should go home if I were you.'

'No need for that.' And maybe he was right because already the colour was coming back into the thin face and after all, John was never that healthy looking. Too long spent peering at precious stones through a magnifying glass. 'I may be in for a touch of flu,' he was saying. 'Nothing to worry about.'

Sara wasn't convinced. 'Maybe you should see a doctor? Do you have these dizzy turns often?'

He took a deep breath, straightening his shoulders. 'Don't worry, my dear. I can take care of myself. Been doing it for years. Ah!' He raised a hand to one ear. 'That's my phone. Excuse me.'

★   ★   ★

As Sara had hoped, everything seemed brighter in the morning and she was ready to laugh at her groundless fears. Of course it must have been the cat all along. Quite possibly a whole posse of cats.

She decided to go round and see how John was and discuss this conclusion. It was too early for customers, but she could leave a note; anyone would easily find her. But as she was pinning the paper to the door, she spotted Helen crossing the square, clutching a leather handbag in both hands and with yet another plastic carrier over one arm.

'Oh! Were you going out somewhere? Don't let me stop you.'

'It's fine,' Sara assured her. 'I was only slipping next door. I knew you were coming, but I didn't expect you to have everything finished so early. You must have been up all night.' she gestured towards the window. 'I've cleared a space as you see and made a start, but I may decide to shuffle things round a bit when I see what else you've brought.'

As always, Helen's work was exquisite and Sara smiled her approval. Helen was fidgeting however as Sara tried to discuss possible arrangements. As if her mind was not fully on what they were talking about.

'There!' Sara said at last. 'What do you think?'

'What? Oh, it's lovely. Yes. Thank you so much.' Helen was still clutching her handbag in both hands. 'Sara, I've done it. I have to. I've brought the *Star* for your jeweller friend to look at.'

'Goodness!' Sara blinked at the black leather handbag. Was Helen wise to be carrying it around like this? But no point in upsetting her further and it wouldn't be for long. 'I'm sure you're doing the right thing.' What was the point in keeping it if getting it out of the bank proved such a worry?

'I just wondered — would you come with me please? I thought he might give me a better valuation if I'm introduced by a friend. Don't you think so?'

Would he? Sara didn't think it would make any difference. 'I'm sure John is scrupulously fair with all his customers. But I'll certainly come with you. No problem there.'

They went into the shop and John

was behind his counter as usual, seemingly completely recovered from his ordeal of the night before. Sarah breathed a sigh of relief. She introduced Helen and began to explain, with Helen contributing a series of halting comments and eventually faltering to a standstill.

John, bless him, understood at once. 'Shall we go through to my office?' Lowering his voice discreetly, even though the shop was empty. 'We'll be more private there.'

Helen mumbled her thanks as he ushered them into what in Sara's shop was a tiny kitchen area. Sara didn't want to intrude on the conversation. With the introduction accomplished, she gazed around the room, deliberately occupying herself with other thoughts even though Helen had asked her to come. Interesting just how different the layout in this shop was, but of course, John had the benefit of a rear extension, with a back door leading to a private parking area. And his stairs were further back.

John however was maintaining perfect discretion, writing the value down on a piece of paper, which he then folded and placed inside a sealed envelope. 'There's no obligation whatsoever, but don't hesitate to come in again if you wish to discuss anything further.'

Helen was glowing with gratitude as they came outside. 'What a very kind man. And he's making everything seem so easy. I'm so glad I had your recommendation. If I have to part with the *Star*, at least I don't have to worry about what to do.'

'If? Have you changed your mind? Do you think you might be able to manage after all?'

'Yes, I was being a bit silly yesterday. Everything was getting on top of me. Maybe I can sell some more of my crafts. And I had a letter this morning telling me about an old post office account I'd forgotten so that will help too, for the moment. At least I know I have the *Star* to fall back on if the house sale doesn't go through quickly. John said there was no obligation, didn't he? And no need to hurry. Well, that has taken a weight off my mind.'

Sara patted her hand. 'That's good. I'm so glad. And if . . . ' She stopped, looking beyond Helen to the clock tower. Didn't she recognise those two vehicles? She had seen them as she passed the protesters' camp the day before, with the large black and silver logos on the sides.

Before she could point them out to Helen, however, a microphone was thrust into their faces and a friendly girl with windswept blonde hair was asking their opinion on the new bypass and the protest.

'I don't know,' Helen said, obviously taken aback. 'Perhaps it seems selfish, but all I want is to get on with my life peacefully.' She was trying to smile but her eyes were flickering nervously.

'That's what everyone wants,' Sara said quickly. 'And although we all value the woodland, the protest may be very unpleasant for local residents. I'm sorry, that's all we're saying just now. We're very busy.' She put an arm around Helen and hurried her away.

Sara saw Helen safely installed in her car, waved her off and stood back to admire the new window display. Yes, if she said it herself, it did look good. It was certain to generate much-needed sales for Helen.

'Could I have a word?'

Oh, no. Sara knew that voice. Her heart sank. And why did she feel so guilty? This was her window. It was true that several months ago, Sara had tried to hint that she couldn't cope with the endless flows of goods Celia produced. Whenever an all-too-rare sale was achieved, Celia seemed to be on the spot immediately with half a dozen more items.

Sara had had to instigate some ground rules and had offered the window slot to soften the blow, but surely Celia couldn't have expected that to last forever? 'Hello, Celia,' she said brightly, blinking at Celia's chosen outfit of emerald and cerise stripes with a tangerine coloured jacket.

Celia's voice was anything but bright. 'I thought we had an agreement about the window?'

'Certainly we did. But it was never intended to be permanent. I was very glad of your work when I first opened, but now I'm really pushed for space.' She added mildly, 'Other people are entitled to have their things in the window too.'

Sara's eyes kept returning to the riotous colours. She wished she had her sunglasses to hand. Not that it would matter how eccentric Celia looked if only she could manage to bring a rainbow-coloured atmosphere with her. I wouldn't be asking for outright happiness, Sara told herself. Pleasant would do. That would be just fine. 'Sorry?'

'I would have thought - as one of your best suppliers - that I would deserve better than this.'

'You are indeed, Celia. A very reliable and prolific supplier. But I have to be fair. Everyone deserves a chance.'

'If you didn't have that ridiculous 'ten items only' rule, I could bring far more.' Celia peered into the window, pointing one finger and obviously counting. 'I knew it. Fifteen! What about the 'ten items only' rule for this person, whoever she is? Because it's evident that these have all been made by the same person. And I can't see why you made the decision to give her all this space — they're so dull and drab.'

Sara took a deep breath. Be tactful. Don't hurt her feelings. For John's sake. 'Many of my customers do appreciate subtle tones. And Helen — this lady — sells extremely well. By the end of the week, she'll be well within the guidelines.'

'I see.' Celia narrowed her eyes. 'It's one rule for me and another for other, less deserving people but who are obviously more favoured in your eyes. And after all John's done for you . . . '

That did it. Sara couldn't bear to hear Helen described as less deserving. Who was Celia to make that judgement? And when she didn't even know her. 'Of course I appreciate everything John's done. It was because of John that I took your work in the first place. Because it isn't always up to the required standard, you know.' Sara put a hand over her mouth, aghast at herself. Too late.

Celia was red in the face. Perhaps she would storm off in a huff, taking her things with her? Sara pushed the thought away. No, whatever the provocation, she wouldn't want to part with Celia like that.

'I'm sorry,' she said quickly. 'I shouldn't have said that. Or I shouldn't have come out with it so abruptly because sometimes I do get the impression you've completed things in a bit of a rush. But I was more than grateful for the display of your work when I was starting out.

'Look, you do still have a very good position. Very eye-catching. No-one will overlook them.' Couldn't possibly, because they were so blazingly bright. Every colour the rainbow had never even thought of. 'If you go and check from beside the clock, I'm sure you'll find you can see them even from there.'

'Humph,' Celia answered. 'This should have been my shop, you know, your landlord made the wrong decision if you ask me.' She turned and set off towards one of the narrow alleys which would take her round to the rear of John's shop, without bothering to follow Sara's suggestion.

Sara stared after her, biting her lips. She had meant to be so tactful, but Celia had the knack of rubbing her up the wrong way. And what on earth had she meant when she'd said it could have been her shop? Sara had had no idea Celia had even wanted it. Maybe she could have a proper talk with Celia.

Explaining matters in terms of customer choice and product flow to make it sound less personal.

Or she could try putting the problem to John and suggesting he might have a word with his sister. She didn't like to think of Celia being upset.

And yes, she must make a resolve to keep the shop open at all times during the stated hours now that the new display was in place. She must make an extra special effort for Helen.

Was that the phone? Unlikely to be a customer at this time of the morning but you never knew. She welcomed the distraction with relief. 'Good morning. The Craft Shop?'

'Sara Dent?'

She had been about to add, 'How can I help you?' But there was something about the voice . . . The words died in her throat.

'Keep out of it. Keep out of what doesn't concern you. Or you'll be sorry.'

4

Sara dropped the phone as if it had been red hot. She was shaking all over. No need to wonder who might be responsible. And now she must definitely call the police. She reached for the handset and hesitated. What about John? He must have had a similar threat from the group in the square. And if so, better if they made a joint complaint.

Sidelining her new resolution about staying open, she set off. This was an emergency and fortunately John was outside. He had the *closed* sign on his door and was bringing his metal shutters down. Oh, yes, Sara thought, it's Tuesday. Although hardly anyone bothered about the traditional half-day now and Sara couldn't afford to lose so much opening time.

He frowned when she told him what had happened. 'No, I haven't had anything like that.' He shook his head. 'I wouldn't go to the police, Sara. Certainly I would avoid accusing those young men. You don't have enough evidence.'

Sara agreed reluctantly. 'I suppose if I did, they could make trouble for you. They might think you had implicated them. And that wouldn't be fair.' All the same, she thought, she would be happier informing somebody official.

'Perhaps it isn't them at all.'

Sara laughed in surprise although she had never experienced anything less funny. 'It has to be, John. Who else could it be? What else would I have to keep out of? It doesn't make sense'

John shrugged, as if he didn't feel much like talking.

'But what am I thinking of? You haven't bothered with Half-Day all summer. Is it that flu again?'

'Flu? Oh, yes. It could be.'

'Don't worry.' She seemed to be encouraging everyone not to worry these days. 'I won't bother the police with something so trivial. Absolutely no point.' But if anything else happened, she resolved, her phone would be bouncing, she would hit it so fast.

At least, the autumn sunshine brought some tourists out and she sold two of Helen's cushions straightaway. Somebody even expressed an interest in something of Celia's, but wanted to haggle. And Celia was always inflexible on price. Still, it was encouraging.

It wasn't until mid-afternoon that Sara had any more time to mull over the phone call problem. By then she felt able to share in John's point of view. Perhaps it was merely a random crank call, she told herself. They wouldn't even have known which buttons they were pushing. Yes, that would be it.

She was beginning to allow herself to relax when the shop bell rang again and here was Celia, with a large blue sports bag. That could only mean one thing, but it was probably best to pretend she hadn't noticed.

'Hello, Celia, I'm glad you've popped

in. I was thinking it might be a good idea to sit down together and talk things through. We both got a bit heated this morning. Would you like a coffee? And I've got some new chocolate biscuits in — you know, those crunchy ones they've been advertising?' She stopped, unable to interpret Celia's expression.

'No, I won't stop long. But don't worry, I never take offence. I understand perfectly that management skills only come with experience.' Celia smiled briefly without parting her lips. 'However, I've decided to collect my things. Easier all round I feel. My action will benefit your understated window display.' She spoke in a sarcastic tone.

'Oh. Are you sure?' Sara knew that she should protest, but couldn't quite bring herself to do that.

'Certainly. I always know what I'm doing. At some point in the future, if you should find that your customers are enquiring about the lack of my craftwork in your shop, then who knows? I may reconsider. But for the moment, I think a short break would benefit both of us.'

'I see,' Sara said. That would explain the smile, she supposed. Celia obviously thought that she would be placing Sara in an uncomfortable position. But already, Sara was planning what she could do with the extra space. 'Yes, I could manage to fill the gap without too much trouble,' she said, carefully.

'Sometimes I think I have more craft workers than customers.' She didn't want to give Celia the wrong impression. If Celia thought that Sara would soon be begging her to return, she would be very disappointed. 'I think I should have foreseen that situation and perhaps instigated a system of rotation from the beginning.'

Celia was already reaching into the various displays and wrapping her embroidered fish-shaped pincushions in tissue paper. 'You can't be too careful, can you? Delicate work such as this can be so easily spoiled.'

'That's true. And you do work so hard, Celia. That's always been evident.'

'Goodbye now,' Celia was saying, almost cheerily. Smiling again. Two smiles in one day. Less than half-an-hour in fact. The world must be tilting on its axis.

Sara's major feeling was of a deep and joyous relief. Perhaps she would prepare a tactful little speech about customer requirements to be ready for Celia's eventual return. And for now, she could have fun rearranging everything.

She looked round the shop, wondering just which items to put in Celia's empty spaces. As much as possible would be good. Let everyone benefit from this windfall to begin with and she could worry about rotating the window space later.

She drifted off to sleep that night with a sense of satisfaction. Knowing that now the window provided a subtle display of natural earth shades, the colours of driftwood and sand and pebbles.

Her contented dreams were interrupted by bells ringing. As she struggled up on to one elbow, her hand — working ahead of her fuddled brain — was reaching for the phone. A wave of panic swamped her. Would she be hearing that harsh, threatening voice again? Had they found out where she lived?

'This is the police, Miss Dent. There has been an incident in your shop and the alarm is going off. If you could come at once? In the interests of security.'

The police. So they'd become involved after all, she thought muzzily. She would have to explain that to John. He would be thinking she'd phoned them and after she'd assured him she wouldn't.

Her heart was thudding as she drove through the silent streets. They had never had trouble like this before. Beckthwaite had always seemed such a quiet little town when she had taken the shop on. Everything was changing.

She parked any old where because apart from the police car, the market square was completely empty. Her whole being was concentrated on the broken shop window and the shards of broken glass littering the pavement. And inside the shop, too. How lucky that John had his metal shutters and had been saved all this.

She unlocked the door and stepped inside, followed by the two policemen. Oh, no. She felt sick. Everything would be ruined. You couldn't sell toys and cushions if there was a risk they might contain slivers of glass. And the thieves had even let loose with spray cans of purple and green paint. Everybody would be devastated. And particularly Helen, who needed the money most of all. She could hardly bear to think of Helen's reaction.

'Who could have done this?' she asked, more or less speaking to herself. 'Why? I don't keep money in the shop. Not that there ever is very much.'

The PCs shrugged sympathetically. 'Vandalism. There doesn't have to be a reason.'

'No, I suppose not.' Apart from Helen and of course, Celia, her little army of craftspeople worked so slowly. How long would it be before she could build up her stock again?

One of the PCs was picking up a large brick. 'That's what they used initially. But they've done more than simply throwing this. Someone's attacked your window with something heavy by the look of things. Really enjoyed making a meal of it.'

Sara opened her mouth to ask if they would be examining the brick for fingerprints. No, of course they wouldn't. Don't be silly, she told herself. Attacks like this were all too common. And obviously the unthinking people who had done it wouldn't care about the effect they'd had on her. 'When can I get on with tidying up? Do you need to seal everything off and examine the crime scene or anything?'

The policemen shook their heads. 'No, it wouldn't help and there was apparently very little chance of catching those responsible. Most likely to be one random, probably drunken, mishap. And you can get on with clearing up as soon as you like.'

She might as well start on the tidying while she was waiting for the workmen to come and fix the window, she supposed. She didn't feel like sleeping now. Shock, probably. And as she had thought, much of the stock was now un-saleable — even things that had been situated some distance from the window were showing telltale glints.

She had felt so weary as she'd struggled out of bed, but now she knew that sleep was out of reach. Her brain was racing. No point in going home even after the place was boarded up. Not when there was so much to do here. And later if necessary, she could curl up for an hour in the squashy chair at the back of the shop where she displayed dolls and throws.

She sighed. Even though the chair was tucked into the furthest corner, she would have to give it a thorough vacuuming first.

* * *

It was dawn before she finally sank into the deep crimson cushions. Just for five minutes, she told herself. With the window blocked with new plywood panels, the shop seemed dark and unwelcoming.

She had to do something about getting the glass replaced and there were all those phone calls to make to her craftspeople, starting with Helen. More than anyone else, she was dreading telling Helen.

She woke to hear a loud banging on the door. 'Come on, open up. I can see you're there. And your car's outside.'

Sara struggled up, trying to work out where she was and what was happening. She stumbled over to the door. 'Matt!' She blinked at him in surprise.

81

'Whatever's the matter?'

His face was dark with anger. 'How could you? You can't deny it. I know it was you. So what game are you playing?'

Sara struggled with the bolts and the door handle, her fingers refusing to obey her. She was furious and totally mystified. At last the door swung open. She could see and hear Matt now without the protective pane of glass in between them and it was hardly an improvement.

'If you would only calm down,' she said coldly, 'I might begin to have some idea of what on earth you are talking about. Though somehow I doubt it. You're making no sense.'

'No? So what about this?' Eyes blazing he was now brandishing a brick in her face.

Sara stepped back, thinking for one horrified moment that he was about to hit her with it. He must have read the terror in her eyes because he lowered the brick and his voice and once inside, moved away a little, giving her space. 'You can't tell me you don't recognise it,' he said.

Well, yes. It looked remarkably like the brick the police had found amongst the wreckage of her window. But how had Matt got hold of it? She had placed it safely under the kitchen sink, just in case the police did want it for fingerprinting after all.

She said accusingly, 'You've been in again, haven't you? While I was asleep.'

His turn to stare now. 'What? Why would I do that? And anyway, your door was bolted. No, I've been far too busy trying to calm Uncle Paul. It was only for his sake that I didn't get hold of the police straightaway.'

He wiped his forehead with his free hand, shaking his head. 'Oh, Sara — he's so fond of you. But, of course, you know that. How could you do this to him? And why? He's always been good to you.'

'Yes, he has. I'd be the first to agree.' Sara found that she was shaking her head in time with Matt's. She was fully awake now, but it didn't seem to be helping much. She was denying something, but wasn't sure what. 'Matt, stop. You'll have to tell me what's happened. Has Mr P been hurt in some way?'

'As if you didn't know.' His face was like steel. 'OK, I'll go along with the act for the moment. But don't think you're getting away with it.'

He stopped, biting his lips together. 'Look. I'll start again. I know something must be troubling you, to make you act like this. I should be interpreting your actions as a cry for help. And I'm willing to ensure that you receive help. But please leave my uncle out of this. He's too old and frail to cope with it.'

Sara took a deep breath. She was clenching her fists in frustration. 'To cope with what?' She felt like shrieking at him. 'Will you please tell me?'

He held the brick up between them, as if it were Exhibit A. 'This brick. Which you tossed through his front window very early this morning. And at a time when I couldn't be with him. But, of course, you'd found that out. Somehow or other.'

Sara was too shocked to speak at first. At last she managed to say, 'But I wouldn't. Ever. Especially not to Mr P.' She swallowed hard, shivering at the injustice of the accusation. 'Why on earth should you think it had anything to do with me?'

Matt gestured back towards the still open door. 'Your car. It was seen. You must have forgotten how distinctive it is. There can't be two like that, surely?'

'No, there aren't.' Sara shook her head. 'I had it painted like that to order. But my car hasn't been anywhere since I came over here last night. When the police phoned me.'

'And the police can corroborate that?'

'Obviously.' She had to work this out. He had to believe her. She couldn't bear the thought of Mr P thinking she would be capable of something like this.

'And don't you see? The same thing has happened to me, too. Hadn't you noticed?'

He seemed to be looking round at the darkened shop for the first time. No doubt he'd been so busy with his own angry feelings that he hadn't paid any attention to her window. 'You've got it boarded up.'

'Go to the top of the class. First prize for observation.'

He said, doubtfully, 'You could have attacked your window yourself. As a cover.'

'No way. Absolutely not. If I'd even contemplated doing something like that, I'd have chosen the glass in the door and made a lot less mess.' She pointed to the unhappy heap of bin bags. 'Just look at that. All my stock is in those bags — ruined. And these things don't even belong to me. I sell them on behalf of other people.

'My first job for this morning is to get on the phone and apologise to them all. And that's going to be horrible.'

She glared at him. 'And the second job is to try and find a glazier when I can't afford one because I can't carry on any kind of business with the window as it is. Even if I had anything much to sell. The whole thing's a nightmare. And I'd just like you to tell me, Mr Clever — why would I wreck my own shop and go through all this hassle? To provide some kind of cover story? That's ludicrous.'

'It doesn't make much sense, I agree.' He was staring at her with his eyes narrowed as if he was trying to believe her. 'But if it wasn't you, why is my uncle convinced that he saw your car at five o'clock this morning?'

'My car?' Suddenly Sara was certain that she knew what had happened. 'It must have been stolen. Someone's taken it.' She pushed aside and ran out into the square.

'Oh, it's there, all right. It was the first thing I looked for when I got here.'

'No, it isn't. It's gone. Oh!'

She followed where his finger was

pointing. 'But I didn't park it there. That isn't my usual parking place.' She turned to face Matt, convinced of what must have happened. 'Someone took it, drove to your uncle's house and then brought it back.'

'Joyriders, you mean?'

'Yes. Isn't it obvious?'

'And then brought it back here? To the square? Considerate joyriders you have round here.'

Sara hesitated. 'What other explanation could there be?'

'You tell me.'

She sighed in exasperation. 'I really don't need this, Matt. I've enough to worry about as it is. And I think it's time you left. Because what motive could I possibly have for victimising Mr P? He's been wonderful to me from day one. I regard him as a good friend and I would never do anything to hurt him.'

Matt was staring at her. 'I would like to believe you. This whole mess is becoming very unpleasant. But at present, I don't see how I can.'

'So for the present, there's nothing more to say,' Sara said icily. 'If you don't mind, and since I've been victimised myself, whatever you think, I have a lot to do.'

He nodded and walked off, taking a distinct interest in her car as he passed it. Sara felt like screaming. As she began to calm down she realised that she was missing the point herself. Her own and Matt's anger and frustration were minor compared with the effect all this must be having on poor Mr Peasholm.

She hated knowing that he thought she must be responsible. And as soon as possible, she must go and see him and put things right. But how? She needed proof.

Easier said than done. And now Matt was out of the way, she had better check her car to make sure it was all right. And if someone had borrowed it, there might be telltale signs.

But the car looked just as usual. No sign of any forced entry or usage although that didn't prove anything because skilled criminals could break in within minutes.

The police had told her they would be keeping an eye but be realistic, they wouldn't be driving past all the time. Once every hour or so if they could manage it.

A pity she didn't keep an eagle eye on her mileage but, of course, she didn't. She wasn't even sure that she hadn't parked the car here herself. She'd been in such a rush, hadn't she, to get to the shop, answering the police summons? She sat in the driver's seat, thinking back. Perhaps she had put it nearer the clock tower. Why put it way over here by the post office when she'd been in such a hurry?

She sighed. She couldn't be sure — her memories of last night were shaky to say the least — and that was hardly evidence. And just now, she must think about the glazier and Helen.

The phone was ringing as she entered the shop. Drat, she hoped whoever it was wouldn't be too long.

Matt had delayed her enough as it was. Not to mention leaving her thoroughly unsettled, as if she hadn't enough turmoil to cope with.

'Just a reminder,' the familiar voice said. 'Now you've seen what we can do. No police. You've been warned.'

'Wait a minute.' Sara was shouting down the phone. As if being loud would somehow make a difference. 'Who is this? What do you mean? And the police contacted me!' But the harsh voice had gone. Again. Wouldn't you know it? It must be whoever was responsible for the window. But why do something like that if this mystery person wanted to avoid police attention? It didn't make sense.

Unless it was purely an act of malice and the whole thing had been intended to frighten her. It had been pretty successful in that case, she'd have to admit. But who would want to? She didn't have any enemies. Unless — she swayed against the counter, her heart thumping. What about Matt?

Did he count as an enemy? He'd seemed suspicious of her friendship with Mr P from the first. But he wouldn't surely go to these lengths — scaring poor Mr P half to death in order to target her. But hang on a minute; she only had Matt's word for it that Mr Peasholm had been a victim.

She sighed in exasperation. If Matt did turn out to be at the bottom of this, she would wipe the floor with him. Wouldn't she just? But for now, she had more urgent matters to consider. Helen, for starters.

Helen's voice was indistinct as she answered the phone. 'Oh, Sara. Thank goodness it's you. I don't know which way to turn.'

'Why? Whatever's the matter?' Sara's heart was sinking rapidly. She was sure that Helen had been crying.

'The police have only just left. It's been dreadful. I tried to phone, but you were engaged — oh, Sara, it's the *Star*. It's been stolen.'

5

'I'll come at once,' Sara said. She could maybe phone Daisy and Jenny and the others from her mobile once she got to Helen's. Poor, poor Helen. Just when she had decided that she didn't need to sell the jewel after all. At least there would be the insurance.

Helen opened the door on the chain and peered round. Her eyes were red-rimmed and her face looked drained and weary. 'Thank you so much for coming. I didn't know who else to ask or what to do.'

Sara gave her a hug. 'Never mind. Here I am.' She looked round the drawing room, surprised that every-thing seemed just as usual. 'Did they make much mess?'

'Not at all. It was as if they knew exactly where to look and what to look for. The police think I was targeted.

That was what they called it.' She nodded.

'Did you tell anyone you would be getting it out of the bank? I'm sorry — I'm sure the police have gone through all this already.'

'I've been trying to remember. I've to get back to the police if I think of anyone else. There was you of course and your jeweller friend and one or two others he recommended. And then the lovely young woman at the bank — and there was that man with the insurance company when I was telling him I couldn't afford to renew the premium.'

'Helen!' Sara stared at her in horror. 'It hasn't run out?'

'Last week. I think that's what he said. But we agreed that it would be safe enough in the bank while I sought other quotations. That's what he suggested.' She hesitated. 'But I think I did say that I might sell — and I laughed and said of course I would have to get it out to do that.'

'I'm sure the police will be getting on

to everyone you've mentioned.' Including me, Sara thought gloomily. At least she had a cast iron alibi for much of the previous night. Although her car didn't seem to have one.

'Yes, they were so nice. Very thorough. I told them no one ever usually came near this place, but at the moment everything's different so I think they're interviewing the people in the protest camp.'

'I suppose they'll have to. But the protesters haven't been bothering you, have they?'

'Not really. I found some in the garden yesterday and when I asked them what they wanted, they said they'd like to buy some milk. So I gave them a pint — I had some left over as it happened.'

Sara didn't like the sound of this. 'How did they seem? Were they snooping around the place?'

'No, they were very pleasant and polite. Oddly dressed you know, but I didn't feel at all threatened by them.

And anyway someone who seemed to be in charge drove up and told them he would give them money for milk, that they must use the shop in the village. A very pleasant young man and with plenty of money, judging by the vehicle he had. One of those expensive four wheel driving ones.

'He was very friendly and reassuring. Telling me all about himself and how he'd just come back from America. In fact, I felt a lot happier about the camp having met him. A great deal safer. And then this happens.'

Four wheel drive. Just back from America. It couldn't be, could it? Sara didn't know what to make of this new development. Why would Matt be hanging around the protesters' camp? Indeed, seemed to be organising it if Helen had got things right.

Unbidden ideas were squirming up into Sara's imagination. Supposing Matt had organised the window break-ins as some kind of a distraction for the overworked police?

If they were running round chasing hapless shop owners, they wouldn't be on the look-out for would-be thieves. The way would have been wide open for breaking in to Helen's house. No, that was wild. Had to be. But once she had formed the thought, it refused to go away.

'But I mustn't keep you any longer,' Helen said. 'Silly of me to ask in the first place. How can you be selling my wares when you're here?'

Sara felt the colour draining from her face. 'Um — yes.' No good. It had to be done. She took a deep breath. 'I'm so sorry, Helen — ' She held Helen's hands and explained as quickly as possible. 'That was why I was phoning you.'

To her surprise, Helen seemed to rally. 'And here am I dragging you over here and monopolising your time when you have problems enough of your own. No, you must get back straightaway and get everything sorted out.'

'I can't leave you here alone.'

'I shall be fine. And they won't come back, will they? They have what they came for.'

'Would you like to stay in my flat tonight?' Sara spoke on impulse.

'I don't think I should leave the house. I must sell now and quickly. If I leave it standing empty, anything could happen to it. I can't take that risk.'

'In that case, I shall come and stay here.' Sara said firmly. 'Don't you worry. I'll come round as soon as I close up tonight. And now I really had better go.'

'Of course you must. And I shall cook you something special. I shall enjoy having someone to cook for.' Helen's brave smile wasn't fooling either of them.

Sara left, resolving to close the shop early if she could arrange everything in time. Let's face it, she had nothing much to sell anyway.

★ ★ ★

Matt leaned forward, scanning his uncle's anxious face. 'Sara tells me she had nothing to do with it. And I'm inclined to believe her.' And not only because by now he was liking the girl more and more and wanted to trust her.

Mr Peasholm shook his head. 'Are you sure? What about the car? I saw it. I know I did.'

Matt explained. 'Sara thinks someone else took it, drove it over here to break your window and then put it back in the square.' He watched as conflicting expressions flickered in his uncle's eyes. Doubt, relief, followed by further doubt. He wished Uncle Paul would share his thoughts with him. Matt was becoming ever more certain he was holding something back.

'You see, Sara has suffered an identical attack. Whoever it was even used a similar brick to ours. I can't see why Sara would do something like that.'

His uncle nodded. 'No, she wouldn't.'

Matt paused, expecting the inevitable

question. It didn't come. So did that mean his uncle already knew the answer? 'Uncle Paul,' he said gently, 'is there something you're not telling me?'

Uncle Paul put his hand to his chest. 'Don't ask me. Please, Matthew. If we just wait a while, everything will be fine, I promise you. I should have managed on my own for a while longer, I see that now. It was too soon to be dragging you into my muddled affairs.'

Matt took a breath. 'Does Sara have anything to do with this, whatever it is?'

His uncle hesitated, looking down at his hands, which were smoothing the crease in his trousers. 'No, I don't think so.'

Matt was still worried about the car. 'Is there someone who would want us to think Sara is involved? And is it connected with whatever is going on over the shop?'

Uncle Paul was gasping with agitation. 'Leave it, Matthew, please. A week or so more. That's all I ask.'

Matt sat back. He couldn't press his

uncle further. The old man would be making himself ill. Easier if Uncle Paul would tell him all he knew of his own volition, but Matt would have to discover the truth for himself and in his own way. 'It's OK. I won't mention this again. Don't worry.'

As Sara had expected, the phone calls were far from pleasant — even though everyone was kind and sympathetic. One or two said they would like to collect straightaway, to see whether anything could be rescued from the damage. 'Better for you anyway,' Jenny said bracingly. 'You won't want a pile of bin bags cluttering your floor space.'

And Sara had to admit that this was all too true. 'Thank you for being so understanding.'

It was not Jenny — or even Daisy or Agnes — who was to be her first visitor however.

When the doorbell rang and Sara turned to see who was waving at her from beyond the *Closed* sign, there was the one person she least wanted to see.

'Celia.' She was tempted to shake her head in dismissal, but of course, she couldn't do that.

She opened the door, smiling ruefully. No way was she going to betray her real feelings. 'You'll have heard I expect? Perhaps I should be investing in some metal shutters like your brother has.'

'My dear, this is dreadful.' Although her face was suitably sorrowful, Celia couldn't seem to help sounding pleased with herself. 'I had to come and see if there was anything I could do to help.'

Behind her, a police car pulled up outside. Sara frowned. What could they want? Were they coming here? Had they discovered who was responsible for the vandalism? But without a glance in her direction, the two PCs were going into John's shop. Oh, dear. She hoped this development wouldn't antagonise the mystery phone voice. 'Sara?' Celia's voice sounded distant.

Sara gave herself a mental shake. 'Not really. I've pretty well got all the clearing up done.' She gestured at the ruined paintwork. 'As you see, it isn't just the broken glass. It's so fortunate you'd already taken everything of yours.' Wasn't it just? The others had all been so understanding.

Celia's possible reaction wouldn't bear thinking about. Oh, no. Another thought struck her. Celia had offered to help. But she couldn't mean that. Surely not. Sara hoped her face wasn't showing the horror she felt. She made an iron bid to control her expression. Because if Celia offered to fill the empty space, she didn't know what she was going to say.

Celia was smiling openly now. 'You'll be needing replacement stock and as soon as possible.' She paused.

'Oh, I don't know. Better get cleaned up properly first. I haven't even got a glazier sorted. And then there's new paint. And everything.' Did she sound convincing?

Celia patted her hand. 'Unfortunately, Sara, only last night I promised a very dear friend that I would display my work at her charity craft fayre on Saturday. She was so grateful. I couldn't possibly let her down. You do understand, don't you?'

'No, you couldn't,' Sara gasped. She had a feeling that Celia was playing with her, but there wasn't much she could do about it.

'After that — and if there's anything left because it is a very well supported fayre — well, we'll see. I may be able to help you out.' Celia sank down into the squashy armchair, seemingly unaware of how badly the vivid red of her floral skirt clashed with the upholstery.

'That's extremely kind of you. I'll bear it in mind. But I wouldn't want to be depriving you of alternative opportunities.'

'Well I can't think of any at the moment, but one never knows, does one?'

No, Sara thought, one doesn't. And surely I can find some more autumn fayres and make sure Celia knows about them. A flier or two through her letter box. John could tell me her address. That should distract her nicely. She shook her head.

Celia was stroking the chair's velvety arms. 'I've always loved this you know. How lucky that it escaped the attack. And if you were willing to part with it, I'm sure I could make you an acceptable offer.'

'Really?' Sara wished she could turn it down. The woman had an annoying knack of looking smug in the face of another's misfortune. With business at a stand still and the rent to think about, Sara couldn't afford to reject the offer but she didn't want Celia to think she was leaping at it. 'I would be reluctant to part with it. I've had it a long time. And it has a sentimental value. But I might be interested. I'll have to think about it.'

Celia stood up. Sara was sure she'd seen straight through her stalling. 'Don't leave it too long. Perhaps we can discuss it further next time I'm passing.'

'Right.' Sara smiled weakly as Celia swept out with a twitch of the scarlet and yellow fabric. She collapsed into the chair — not even hers for much longer, if Celia would agree to a reasonable price. But if she thought she'd be getting it for peanuts, she would be very much mistaken. Sara lay back, closing her eyes.

'Can I come in?'

Her eyes shot open at the familiar voice. Correction — Celia hadn't been the very last person she wanted to see. This was. 'What can I do for you, Matt?' She hadn't thought he would be back so soon. And smiling. Why did that make her feel uneasy?

'I've come to offer apologies. I was well out of order, making unfounded accusations left, right and centre.'

'Yes.' Sara said. 'I mean, it did seem unfair. When I've always liked Mr P so much and wouldn't do anything to hurt him.' Self-evident to her, but what had made Matt change his mind, she wondered?

'And as proof of my sincere repentance, I've come to see if you'd like to borrow our glazier. He's just about finished up at the house.'

'Would I? Oh, yes, please.' Never mind what was driving Matt, just grab the offer while it was going. The change in him was unbelievable. So sudden that it seemed too good to be true. No, that wasn't quite fair. He did look as if he meant what he said.

'Don't go away,' he called over his shoulder, leaping out to speak to someone in a blue van. Obviously the glazier must be here on the spot already. That was service for you.

For the next half hour or so, Sara felt as if she were in a soft and cosy dream as Matt took charge — in the nicest possible way and deferring to her opinion wherever necessary. She could have managed on her own of course; she was used to doing everything herself since the break up with Tony but she would have to admit that this was all very pleasant.

And this meant also that she was able to concentrate fully on the craft workers when they arrived. Their ready sympathy and understanding made her feel that she wanted to cry. Reaction, she thought, after the long tiring night but she would have coped with anger better.

She wondered also why Matt still seemed to be hanging around. The glazier was obviously very competent. Matt didn't stand over him; at one point she noticed from the corner of her eye that the police constables were making a return visit next door and Matt was wandering over to chat to them as they were leaving.

After that there was no time to think about Matt for a while because the policemen were coming over to speak to her. Routine enquiries, they told her, about a recent theft in the area. Of course, they wanted her to corroborate what Helen had told them about her intentions of selling the *Star*. That explained why they had been to see

John too. Their questions were straight-forward and didn't last long. By the time the window was finally restored, they had been gone for some time. Whereas Matt was still hanging around.

She didn't care whether Matt was still there or not. At last she could feel that things were returning to normal. She breathed a sigh of relief, regarding the sheet of glass with satisfaction and realising suddenly that Matt was out by the van giving a cheery wave as the engine spluttered and roared.

'Hey.' Sara ran out as the van swept away. 'Does he know what to put on the bill? My business name?'

'No need to worry about that,' Matt said easily. 'Landlord's responsibility.'

'I'm sure it's nothing of the sort. It wouldn't be fair to expect you to foot this. It's hardly normal wear and tear. And I should be able to get it back off the insurance.' She crossed her fingers behind her back. Helen wasn't the only one to be behind with the payments.

'I had a word with Danny, the glazier,

in advance and arranged a good deal. If we call it a block booking, we get better rates. Two for the price of one. Believe me, if you insisted on a separate bill, we'd both lose out.'

'Well, OK. Thank you.' Sara was suddenly almost overwhelmed by a wave of weariness and too tired to argue. She walked back inside, half surprised to realise that Matt had followed her. Surely he would be ready to go now? It had been a long day for everyone. But after his surprising kindness, she could hardly be pushing him off.

'Would you like a cup of tea?' she asked. 'I never thought — should have asked Danny if he wanted another.'

'I'm sure he wanted to get off. He'll have advance bookings to get on with and it was good of him to fit us in. But I'll have one if there's one going, thanks.' He followed her into the kitchen and seemed to be inspecting the small room from top to toe so his next question took her aback. 'Did you report your car being stolen? When you were talking to the police?'

She stared at him. 'No, I didn't think. Though I suppose I should.'

'They didn't seem to have got very far with their enquiries on your behalf.'

'No, I don't expect them to come up with anything. It's just something that can't be helped.' She shivered. 'Now you know what we can do.' Nothing like Matt's voice. But voices could be disguised.

'Besides, those weren't the same policemen. My two will be safely off the night shift and tucked up in bed by now. No, they were asking about a robbery that happened last night, when a valuable piece of jewellery was stolen.' She was concentrating on the kettle as she spoke so she didn't have to look at Matt. This would be the opportunity for him to tell her that he had met Helen himself.

She made her voice casual. 'In fact, the jewel belongs to a friend of mine. She lives in that large house between

111

the woods and the bypass.' She waited for him to make the natural following-on statement — telling her why he had been up at the protest camp.

He was looking at his watch. 'I'm really sorry — hadn't realised what time it was. There's something I have to sort out.' He reached past her, slurped some milk into the mug and took a couple of mouthfuls. 'But I wanted to tell you, if you should find this is getting too heavy and want to get out, I won't hold you to anything. After all this, I don't think it would be fair.'

'What?' At first, Sara couldn't think what he meant.

He was already opening the door. 'Renting the shop. It's a lot to worry about when you're on your own.'

'Oh, no. Goodness, no, it would take a lot more than this to frighten me.' If she said it out loud, in that very confident way, she might begin to believe it.

He nodded. 'Let me know if you change your mind. Any time. Oh, nearly forgot. Could I have my key back please? For upstairs?'

Sara stared at him, not knowing why her heart was suddenly pounding. Because of course he could have it.

Hadn't she originally intended to return it straightaway? She didn't know why she was experiencing a feeling of reluctance. 'I'm sorry,' she heard herself saying. 'I left it at home — with rushing over here in the middle of the night . . . '

'Oh. I see.'

'I took it home with me for safety. I'll bring it in with me tomorrow. Will that be OK?'

'Right. Yes.' He didn't seem too pleased.

'I could go now and get it for you, if you like.'

'No. It's OK. Like I said, I haven't time. Tomorrow will do.' The grey eyes were staring at her. Sara flushed, wondering if he could see through her excuses and knew she wasn't sure whether the key was here or not. But she did know that she wanted to get a copy made before giving it back.

There were just too many inconsistencies, too many topics of conversation where she kept getting the impression that Matt was concealing something. There was something strange going on and it was time that she found out exactly what it was.

6

It was a long afternoon when she felt she might as well get on with the rest of the clearing up, but with that accomplished she sank down in the chair. Only for five minutes, she promised herself but before she knew it, she was opening her eyes to discover that the afternoon had gone.

In fact, if she was going to get the key copied, there was only just time to nip along to Kevin's Shoe Repair and Key Cutting shop on the north side of the square. Right, that was what she would do. Decision made. No time like the present. She snatched up her bag. Ah. Perhaps the present wouldn't be the best time after all. Because there was Matt, still parked near the clock tower. Surely he couldn't have been out there all afternoon. What was he doing?

Nothing much as far as she could

see. He was sitting in the driver's seat and staring ahead and not in her direction, fortunately, but she felt uneasy all the same. What could he be planning? And how long was he going to sit there? She wanted to get this over and done with.

An idea struck her. Perhaps the best way of concealing her actions would be to make them as open as possible. How about taking something in for soling and heeling? She looked down at her black low-heeled shoes. They could probably do with it. An excellent smokescreen. You couldn't tell that Kevin did key cutting until you were a couple of feet away from his shop window. And she had some old sandals she could wear instead, in the tiny coat cupboard.

That was good; John was standing in his doorway. She waved the black shoes in front of him, resisting the urge to look round and make sure Matt was watching. 'Just popping to Kevin's for five minutes. Silly, isn't it? I feel I have to lock up now, even though there's nothing inside.'

He nodded in sympathy. 'I know what you mean. But I'll be keeping an eye out anyway. You carry on.'

Sara set off along the pavement and almost immediately remembered why the sandals had been shoved in the cupboard. The left one was flapping off her foot as she walked, making her limp. Perhaps she would get the sandals mended instead.

Mustn't glance over to the clock. Mustn't hurry - though she couldn't anyway.

She limped along the pavement, wincing as a cold draught of wind swept through the narrow alleyway at the corner with a stench of dustbins and rotting rubbish. In spite of everything she had on her mind, she looked upwards, as she always did at this point. Above her, the two narrow windows overlooked the alley, facing each other. They were known as the lover's casements according to Kevin.

An eager young apprentice in the Middle Ages had leapt across the gap each night to meet his beloved, grasping a rope of knotted sheets. Until the rope failed and he fell to an untimely death. No wonder the alley felt so cold.

As Kevin said, every shop in the square held a story but she had scurried past the empty shop where the Frank Chesters robbery and murder had occurred. Somehow, that unit was never occupied for long.

At last. She was there. Shoe Repairs and Keys Cut. She closed Kevin's door behind her with a sigh of relief. 'You can leave that open if you would,' Kevin Hays said cheerfully. 'Gets very stuffy in here.'

'Oh. All right.' She had seen the door as a welcome barrier. But surely Matt wouldn't be able to see right inside the shop? Not at this distance? She risked a quick glance in his direction and gave an exclamation of annoyance. He'd gone.

While she had been performing this

mini-drama for his benefit, he had lost interest in her. She almost felt disappointed — which was ridiculous. But she hadn't thought Matt would be the sort to give up so easily. No need for the shoe charade at all. She bent down and slid her feet back into her black shoes with relief.

'So what can I do for you?' Kevin was gazing at her with concern, his head tilted on one side. She couldn't blame him.

'Oh, I'd like a key cutting, please.' She realised that Kevin was looking at the sandals in her hand. 'No, these are too old to bother with. I've realised that on the way over. And the black ones don't really need it yet. So just the key. That will be fine.'

Kevin was searching on the rack for a suitable blank. 'This will do it. Unusual key though, isn't it? You don't get too many of these nowadays. Lucky you came to me as it's a specialist job.'

'Yes. I hadn't thought about that.' Sara wasn't too keen on the way the conversation was going. He would be asking where the key had come from next. She made a point of taking a deeply appreciative breath. 'I always love the smell of your shop. So leathery.' But the shelves were filled with other useful items too such as clotheslines and light bulbs.

'Leather and machine oil,' Kevin said. His expression changed. He was looking over her shoulder out into the square. 'You haven't left your shop open, have you?'

'No — and anyway John's there.' she turned to look at the square. 'Oh, I see what you mean.'

'That's right. John's nephew and his little gang are back already. It's a bit early for them. But if John's keeping an eye out for you, you should be all right. And this won't take long.'

Sara looked up from scrabbling in her purse to stare at him. 'Nephew? That lad in the baseball cap is John's nephew? I didn't know. Why ever didn't John tell me?'

Kevin laughed. 'John's a respected member of the community. Would you be happy to admit to having a nephew like that?'

'Well, no. Probably not.' She couldn't quite get her head round this. So did that mean she and John had never been in any real danger from those young men? No wonder John hadn't wanted her to phone the police.

'I happen to know because my mum used to live next door to John and Celia's parents.' Kevin was shouting now, above the noise of the whining machinery. 'John never mentions that either. Not a very salubrious part of town.'

Sara shook her head. You learned something new every day. So was Celia that unpleasant young man's mother? Must be, she supposed. She seemed to remember Celia referring to her divorce once. As she walked back slowly, with the two keys safely in her pocket, she tried to work out what this might mean.

If John knew the youths, it seemed

unlikely they had been responsible for the phone calls and the vandalism. So, where did that leave her? What else could she possibly have to stay out of? There was only one thing she could think of. And that was her friendship with Mr Peasholm.

But how could threats over the phone be expected to achieve that? Well, yes — they might intimidate her in general. So that she might decide to leave the shop altogether. Would that be an advantage to Matt? After all, that was what he had suggested — and she had thought he was trying to be kind. Oh, this was all too complicated. Head scrambling time.

John stuck his head out of his door. 'Back now? You didn't have any would-be customers.'

'Thanks.' Should she tell him she knew about his nephew. She bit her lips. No, maybe that wouldn't be fair. If John had wanted her to know, he could have told her himself, anytime. And no wonder he hadn't wanted the police involved. But from now on, she would let John deal with the group in the square in his own way.

Also, she was going to begin a systematic daily check on the rooms upstairs. As of now. Nothing, from this moment on, would escape her notice. She turned the 'closed' sign round and locked and bolted the door. No surprise visitors this time.

She marched up the stairs, filled with determination. And yes, the rooms were empty and silent. First room, second, third, tiny scullery/kitchen, neglected bathroom. Check the cupboards. Not even any sign of the cat. Though possibly he could be a welcome visitor if he waged war on any other livestock.

As far as she could tell, the marks on the floor had not altered. And perhaps they were ages old anyway. No way of knowing. So that was that. Today's check all done and dusted.

She turned back to the entrance door at the top of the stairs and realised for the first time that there was another cupboard behind it, set into the wall. Once the main door was open, it concealed the cupboard almost completely. OK, she would check it now. She turned the handle, expecting yet another empty, dusty space with spiders scuttling into the corners.

The cupboard was piled high with new cardboard boxes. She peered at the blue lettering and the white labels. CD players, DVD players, even several laptops. As if somebody was setting up an electrical shop. And perhaps Matt did have that in mind, for all she knew. He wouldn't be obliged to tell her — but you would think he'd have mentioned it. She slid the topmost box and shook it gently. Yes, it was certainly full.

She swayed against the doorframe, her heart thumping. Perhaps Matt did have other plans for the shop, if he could persuade her to leave. No wonder he'd wanted her to return the key.

She locked up and went downstairs, almost too angry to think straight. How dare he think he could get rid of her so easily?

Matt's feet were developing cramp with standing still for so long. But he was staying put. He was determined that he wouldn't be shifting until Sara had decided to leave. Somehow he had to discover what was going on.

With the convenient duplicate key from the rusty tin box, he could come and go as he pleased. But he wasn't happy about Sara sharing in that facility. And why did she seem so reluctant to return the key she had 'borrowed'? Finding an opportunity to slip into the shop and check around again had been easy.

She herself had given him the idea of going upstairs while she slept in the chair, and he hadn't been too worried about her waking and finding out; he had every right to be there. But she hadn't woken. As he passed quietly, he had half smiled at the picture she presented, curled up with her hair falling across her face.

He hadn't been smiling when he came down. His first instinct on finding the boxes in the cupboard had been to tackle her straightaway. But she would lie her way out of it. She seemed to have a knack of getting to him with that little-girl-innocent look she could put on. So should he ring the police? The electrical goods had to be stolen. What other explanation could there be? And he didn't want to suspect Sara of anything dishonest but who else could be responsible?

If she was innocent, she would have volunteered the information when they were in the shop together. As her landlord, he had the right to know if anyone did. He shook his head, grimly.

But if she had an explanation, he should at least hear it, he supposed. He sighed. He had to admit it; he desperately wanted Sara to be innocent. And one more thing, he needed to be one hundred per cent certain his uncle wasn't involved in this. Highly unlikely of course, but not a risk he could take.

That was why he was hanging around with his coat collar round his ears and his feet turning to ice.

He needed more information before taking any action and was certain he was on the verge of finding out. Because what was Sara doing there now, well after closing time and with no stock left anyhow? Someone, he reasoned might be arriving soon to remove the goods — or bring more. She must have contacts.

He looked at his watch, wishing she would make a move. He had obligations to think about, places to be, promises to keep. He trusted the others to perform but it was his idea and he would see it through. 'Come on, come on,' he muttered. At last. He stared at the shop with eyes narrowed as the lights went out.

Sara's mobile was chirping. She frowned, hoping whoever it was wouldn't be long because she had told Helen she would be there before dark. Oh, it was Helen. 'It's OK,' Sarah said cheerfully. 'I haven't forgotten our arrangement.

I'm just on my way. Just locking up in fact.'

'That's why I'm ringing.' Helen's voice sounded much happier. 'You don't need to come after all. I've found someone else.'

'Have you?' Sara's first response was relief. That meant she could hang on here and put her plan into operation. But wait a minute. 'I didn't think you knew anyone else?'

'Three young men who will be completely trustworthy, I'm sure. They come with the best recommendations.' Helen's voice died away as the reception faded. Sara shook her mobile impatiently. ' . . . old friends are you know,' Helen was saying.

'Who? I'm sorry, I missed that.' No, the voice had gone again. Never mind, she would try Helen on the shop phone. But now the number was engaged. Either Helen was still trying to make the connection work or she might be finalising her arrangements with these trustworthy young men she'd found. Sara decided to try again later — and it was great to know that Helen had managed to find someone. Nobody would target the house with a group of people there.

So, where was I? I can get back to keeping watch, she thought. Matt'll be along sooner or later, no doubt about that. And when he arrives, I'll be ready. Sara sat back in the chair Celia was going to buy — she might as well enjoy it while she could.

The square was empty now. Even John's nephew and his crew had departed. Her own car was alone in the sea of cobbles. Of course. 'You fool,' Sarah said out loud. 'Some secret watch this is with my car outside to give me away. Matt's hardly going to try anything with that there.'

But that was easily solved. She only had to move it round the back. No problem. She would just have to hope that Matt didn't make a move while she was manoeuvring around the one-way system. She locked the shop and trotted across the square. Or perhaps the car park by the church would be better? A good five minutes walk away but no chance of Matt spotting the car there. Yes, she would do that. She glanced in her mirror and set off.

As she turned out of the square, she almost jammed her brake to the floor. It couldn't be. She was seeing things now. But that sleek shape behind her looked suspiciously like Matt's vehicle. Forget the car park, she must lose him. Her car leapt forwards, narrowly missing a wall. She regained control, picked up speed and made for a long straight stretch leading away from the town.

No, he was still there. Hanging back, hoping she hadn't seen him no doubt. Obviously he had been lying in wait for her. No wonder he'd looked to be so deep in thought that afternoon. He'd been plotting his next move and now he was going to follow her home, making sure she was well out of the way — and then return to the shop to start adding more goods to his secret store. Or whatever.

She drummed her fingers on the steering wheel. Time for a counter-plot. Oh, yes. So you're expecting me to drive home are you, Mr Clever? Right, that was exactly what she would do. She eased her right foot a little. Now she didn't want to lose him. Her street was almost fully parked up as usual but there was one space right outside — good, though two would have been better.

As she got out, Matt was sailing past. She had a moment of panic, fighting the urge to wave. He had noticed, hadn't he? No, it was OK. He was sliding into a space several doors down. Great, because that meant she would be able to see him from her front window.

Mustn't look and see what he was doing but she fiddled with her bag and her keys for longer than necessary to give him plenty of time to see where she was going. She unlocked the outer door and went up the stairs. Usually she loved

131

coming home. She had the flat decorated and furnished exactly as she wanted and she would always make for the kitchen to have a glass of wine or a cup of hot chocolate, depending on her mood and the weather.

Tonight, she put the light on and went to stand in the window, arranging and adjusting the curtains but without shutting them. He must know now that she was safely inside? She went into the bedroom and squinted through that window, leaving the light off. No, he was still there. What would he expect her to do? How long would he stay?

Unfortunately she didn't have time to wait and find out. Now she could close the living-room curtains. And leave them closed while she made her preparations. Jeans, baggy sweater and a woollen hat pulled over the giveaway warm brown curls. And a large shoulder bag containing a camera, her toothbrush and a change of underwear. Just in case this became an allnight vigil.

Whatever it takes, she thought

grimly. He wouldn't realise there was a rear door leading to the shared garden — and if he did, would have no idea about the hole in the fence behind the lilac bushes, which would take her directly to the main road where she could catch the Number 48.

It worked well. Within half an hour, she was sitting safely on the bus and congratulating herself. As the bus turned the corner and passed the end of her own street, she even glimpsed the four-wheel drive still parked hopefully. Good.

She approached the shop with care all the same. No sign of anyone. Not even John, whose shutters were down and locked, the upper rooms in darkness. That was good because John was so vigilant and she wouldn't want him phoning the police too soon. Without the evidence she hoped her camera would provide, Matt would just deny everything.

She curled up in the chair, pulling a warm woollen throw over herself and knowing that for anyone entering the shop, she would be almost invisible. Then minutes passed, slowly. Looking at her watch, she was certain she had been here almost an hour. But no, it was still ticking. Her head began to droop. Perhaps she had let her imagination run away with her. And she was feeling so tired. The excitement of cleverly evading pursuit was wearing off, leaving her with a deep feeling of weariness. You wouldn't think that she'd slept for so much of the afternoon.

Why had this seemed such a good idea? Perhaps all the activity and excitement had affected her judgement. But good idea or not, she was here now and stuck with it, because she was too tired to do anything else.

A tiny click woke her. The sound of a key in the outside lock. For a moment she couldn't remember where she was. It was dark. How long had she been asleep? And now she couldn't hear anything. She peered into the gloom.

Had she imagined that give-away sound? But something was different.

Yes, there was somebody standing at the bottom of the stairs. Waiting and listening, just as she was. She pressed a hand against her mouth. She had been right because in spite of the darkness, she recognised the set of the shoulders and the way he was standing. It was Matt.

7

She shrank back into the cushions and beneath the rug, trying to hold her breath. He was still there. A click as he lifted one arm and a narrow beam of light swung across the shop. He was pausing too long, even though he couldn't possibly see her. Curled up as she was, she would seem to be a heap of fabric. And yes, she heard his footsteps moving slowly up the stairs.

Soundlessly, she took a long slow breath. That was it. The torch proved it. If he'd come here for any straightforward and honest purpose, he would have put the downstairs lights on. She should feel pleased to be proved right she supposed but was only aware of a leaden feeling of disappointment.

As the torch beam flickered upwards and out of sight, Sara eased herself out of the chair and followed. At least sitting in the dark for some time meant that her eyes were used to the gloom and she could see quite well. She had the advantage over Matt that way. Automatically, she checked the outer door as she passed it but Matt had locked it behind him.

She knew exactly where he would be — right behind the upper door, scrabbling about in his cupboard. Any minute now he would be making those distinctive noises she'd been hearing for the past fortnight. And that would be photo time. Snap.

She stood at the top of the stairs for what seemed a long time. What could he be doing? Had he gone through into one of the other rooms? And if so why? She clicked her tongue in annoyance. Why couldn't he behave in the way she'd been expecting?

She couldn't even see the torch beam now through the gap in the open door. But if she edged her head round — because there was just enough room — and yes, there was a beam of light in the kitchen. Immediately in front of her, the mysterious boxes were out of their cupboard, taking up a substantial amount of floor space. She whistled silently. She had been right. Whatever Matt had in mind, he was here to do more of it. And she would get a grandstand view.

And, yes, an even better view from inside the room and behind the propped up planks she'd noticed before. If he stayed in the kitchen a few moments longer, there would be time to edge round the door and hide herself behind them. That way, she would have a one-hundred-per-cent all-round sighting of what went on — and would be able to wait until Matt had left before leaving herself. Because let's face it, she hadn't thought about how she was going to get out of here.

If he was involved in something really heavy, she would be better not giving any sign of her presence here at all. Lucky she'd thought of that in time. And yes — quick glance at the kitchen

— torch still there. She slid through the gap and round the corner to her left, her eyes on the torch beam all the time.

From nowhere, strong hands gripped her wrist and covered her mouth to stifle her scream. Sara was rigid with shock. She wanted to struggle but seemed to have forgotten how. A voice was hissing in her ear. 'What do you think you're doing?'

The freezing sensation melted abruptly. She pulled furiously at Matt's hands, gurgling something indecipherable even to her.

'OK, but don't make any stupid noises.' He took his hand from her mouth but was still gripping her arm. 'Truth time, I think. Who's in this with you?'

'With me? Oh, very clever. Very convincing. When whatever is happening up here involves you one hundred and two per cent. That's obvious.' She glared at him. 'And I want to know what it is.'

Her brain was skimming along ten to

the dozen. He hadn't been thinking of starting up an alternative business at all. Suddenly she knew. 'The goods in the cupboard are stolen! That's it, isn't it? Does Mr Peasholm know about it? Because if you're doing something that's going to cause trouble for him, I'll never forgive you. He's old and defenceless — and when you have to go to court, I'll stick up for him with every last breath.'

She could just about make out his face as he stared at her. 'What? You think that I'm involved?' He shook his head. 'No way. I'd been putting my money on you. You have the opportunity. And a spare set of keys. Why did you make sure you'd kept the key? Another convenient oversight, was it?'

Sara clenched her fists. 'Because I didn't trust you. Because I needed to find out what's going on — to try and protect Mr P. I needed to check up on you.' She closed her eyes, wishing she could get to the bottom of this. She wanted to believe Matt. His concern for

Mr P seemed genuine. But if it wasn't him, who else could it be?

Matt muttered, 'I was convinced you had something to do with all this. But no. It doesn't add up.' He paused. 'Know what? I think I believe you.'

'I should hope so. But I'm not sure that I believe you. Why are you skulking about in the dark?'

He gestured to the boxes. 'I've every right to be here. Something's going on and I need to find out what?

Sara tried to twist round to stare at him. 'You need to find out? Oh, come on. As if you didn't know already.' She was willing him to tell her the truth. In the dim light, his eyes seemed dark and impenetrable.

'I can assure you this is nothing to do with me.' He sighed as at last he let go of her arm. 'OK, let's accept that neither of us is responsible for these boxes. That means someone else must be and from the way this stuff has been left, whoever it is could be arriving at any time. It looks to me as if they're in the middle of something. And they could well be dangerous. You need to get out of here ASAP,' he was speaking with a quiet urgency.

'Just as dangerous for you, surely?'

'I'm not going to confront anyone or do anything foolhardy. Just watch and then notify the police. Besides,' as he glanced at his watch, 'there's somewhere I have to be. I didn't think I'd be here long. And a promise is a promise.'

Those little pieces of conversation were clicking together in Sara's head again. 'Very pleasant young men.' 'One who seemed to be in charge.' 'One of those expensive four-wheel things.' 'It's you,' she said suddenly. 'Isn't it? You've been hanging around Helen, gaining her confidence and now you're supposed to be protecting her.'

All her suspicions were rushing back and in abundance. Concealing stolen goods was bad enough but if he had anything to do with the theft of the Star, she could never, ever forgive him. She bit back a sob, forgetting to be cautious. 'Why have you pushed your-self onto Helen? Do you know something about the burglary?' Oh, please, she thought, her heart thudding, let me be wrong about this.

'Helen? I don't know what you're talking about?'

'If this is a dodge to take anything else of hers in the guise of protecting her, you'll have me to answer to. She's a wonderful person and I won't have her harmed in any way.' She swallowed quickly to prevent the angry tears affecting her voice.

To her surprise, Matt was almost laughing. 'I don't believe this. You were suspecting me of that too? Are you looking after all the elderly people in Beckthwaite single-handed? Not that it comes as a surprise. I'm sure you would if you could.'

'It isn't anything to laugh about. I need to know.'

'Sorry. But again, I had my doubts about you. The police seemed to be taking an interest in you today didn't they? That's why I was speaking to them. And OK, I know it was only routine. But you had me worried there for a while. Again. Look, Sara, I've been specialising in various conservation projects worldwide. I've come back now to share the skills I've learned, wherever I can be of use. I was visiting the protest camp because both sides invited me in. I'm trying to mediate. Sorting out the best solution for the neighbourhood as a whole.'

'Oh, I see.' If only she'd paused to ask the right questions. Instead of being so sure that she couldn't trust Matt because Tony had been untrustworthy.

Yes, the more she considered everything, the more she was certain that, all along, Matt had been telling the truth.

'I discovered that one of my local contacts was an ex-policeman who had to leave the force through ill-health. And his parents were old friends of Helen and her brother. I re-introduced them and he will be on guard duty at

Helen's house tonight. She will be perfectly safe, I assure you. But nevertheless, I promised her there would be at least two of us present at all times and I'm going over myself.'

'I should have trusted Helen's judgement,' Sarah said quietly. 'My mum always used to say that she was an excellent judge of character. I'd forgotten that.'

He put his arms around her shoulders to give her a swift hug. 'You weren't to know. I admire the way you try to protect everyone. Where would they be without you? But I hope if anyone is going to show here tonight that they get a move on. I told Helen half-nine at the latest.'

'Well I don't think anyone will be arriving anywhere when your torch is still in the kitchen. A bit of a give-away.'

'Thanks for pointing that out.' He grinned. 'My trap worked though, didn't it? You fell for it.'

'Very clever I'm sure. But the kitchen will be the ideal place for both of us to wait and see what happens next.' Because if he was still trying to send her away, he could think again. To her relief, he nodded. No doubt he was thinking it would be less trouble to fall in with her suggestion.

She knew suddenly that it was all right and that she could believe Matt. She was more certain of that than she had ever been sure about anything. All her instincts were surging with relief and she felt a foolish urge to giggle. She pushed a fist against her mouth to make herself keep quiet.

There was less room than she remembered in the kitchen. She reached for the torch and Matt reached across her at the same moment and it rolled off the ancient Formica. They both dived to the floor to catch it and collided in a muddle of limbs. Sara was laughing under her breath. Matt's arms were round her. His face was close to hers and somehow she wasn't in any hurry to move away.

She didn't know how long the kiss

lasted. It seemed like forever. She forgot where she was. She only wanted this to go on happening.

From the room behind them, came a sharp click. Sara opened her eyes and knew Matt had heard it too. He moved his head away gently, mouthing 'Ssh.' He didn't need to tell her. Someone else was out there. But how? Sara knew that the downstairs door to the shop was locked. But there was no time to worry about that now.

Silently they untangled themselves and slid to stand behind the kitchen door. In the glow of the street lamps, she could make out two figures by the boxes. There was no need for Matt's warning gesture but she was glad of the warmth of his fingers on her arm all the same. She nodded to show she understood.

The men were talking in low voices. 'Don't see why there has to be all this rush.'

'No, you wouldn't. If you hadn't slung the brick through her window, we

147

wouldn't be in this mess.'

The other mumbled something about warning her off.

'What? Police all over, that new bloke making random checks? You might as well stick posters up. You've wrecked this operation, you know that. He's not pleased.'

'Shut up and get a move on. Watch it!' Those familiar scraping noises, accompanied by assorted swearing and panting.

'Tell you what — I've had it with this. Being ordered about. Used for mugs and paid in peanuts. When we get this lot down, I'm going to put my feet up for five. The old boy might have another bottle of best malt knocking around. Because I think we deserve it.'

'Why wait? Let's go for that now.' The voices died away.

'They've gone,' Matt whispered. 'For now.'

Sara frowned. 'But where have they gone? Our door's still locked. And who's 'the old boy?''

'That's what we'd better find out.' There were now only a few boxes in the room and the cupboard door was wide open. Without the need to speak further, Matt and Sara moved quickly and quietly to peer inside. Sara gasped. They were looking into an open passageway. 'It goes through into the room over John's shop,' Sara muttered.

'Certainly does. And when it's shut, you can't tell it's there from this side.'

'They must be using it without him knowing. Or maybe they're blackmailing him?' No wonder John had wanted to handle the group in the square on his own. 'So what do we do now? Get the police?'

'And tell them what? By the time they get here . . . '

'Right. Even if those two find any bottles of whisky downstairs to occupy themselves with, they'll be long gone by then.' Celia's son and one of his mates, she presumed.

'And we need more than this for the police. We're short on information. My uncle's affairs are in more of a mess than I ever realised and he can't remember half of what he's doing. I've been asking him, gently, but if he can't remember, he gets upset.'

'There might be some quite legitimate arrangement,' Sara said eagerly. 'John may be borrowing the flat for something perfectly legal. And perhaps his nephew is deceiving everyone.'

'Let's hope so,' Matt's voice was grim, as he stepped through the wardrobe. 'You stay here.'

No way. She wasn't going to miss out. Besides, two pairs of eyes would be better in witness statements. Picking her way through the boxes wasn't easy even though the cupboard was only half full now. She was thinking furiously. Perhaps if they tackled John about this? Would that get Mr P off the hook? She took out her camera.

The room was a mirror image of theirs. And just as empty and unused — apart from the boxes that were now in mid-transit. They could hear noises of searching and banging about from downstairs, coming from John's back rooms. Poor John. She hoped his visitors weren't making too much mess. 'Why use our rooms when they've all this room on their own side?' she murmured in Matt's ear.

He shrugged. 'In case the shop was searched?'

Sara had an idea. 'Why don't we take a couple of smaller boxes to the police — they'll be able to check the serial numbers and identify the whole lot?'

He made a thumbs-up gesture. 'Great.' His face stilled. 'Ssh.'

Sara didn't need telling. They were coming back.

The voices were at the bottom of the stairs. 'Miserable old skinflint. You'd think he'd have more than a lousy half bottle.'

There was no time to pick their way past the boxes. They were trapped on John's upper floor. Matt grasped her arm but Sara was moving just as fast. They slide into the equivalent upper kitchen together and just in time.

'Doesn't trust us.'

'Yeah. Always moaning. Never paying us the full whack. Tell you what, it's time for someone else to put a few ideas into the frame. Wants this over and done with, does he? I'll show him who knows how to finish a job off.'

Silence apart from the sound of liquid being splashed about. Sara frowned. Had they found some alcohol after all? So why not drink it? No, she sniffed at the familiar, acrid smell in horror. Petrol.

The rough voice came again. 'And through here.' The sounds of footsteps entering the cupboard and returning. 'I don't know why we're bothering with all this stuff. More money this way — when the insurers cough up.'

'Come off it. I'm taking them downstairs if you're not. We can stow them away for ourselves. He'll think they've gone up with the rest. Neat, eh?'

'Right, that's next door sorted — and puts the blame squarely on them.

That's thinking ahead. I'll show him what I can do, left to myself.' The voice was filled with gleeful triumph. 'Because this will settle a few family scores. No one puts one over on my mum and gets away with it. That craft woman deserves all she gets.'

Celia, Sara thought. Suddenly she understood. The brick and the telephone threats had been in revenge for her moving Celia's things. She felt dizzy for a moment or two. No wonder Celia had seemed so pleased with herself when she took them away. She had known only too well what was going to happen next.

Sara clenched her fists to control her anger. She wanted to rush out and confront the horrible little thugs. How dare they. Beside her, Matt must have been reading her mind because he put a warning hand on her arm. She raised her eyebrows and shook her head to reassure him. She just wished they would hurry up and go.

Matt was trying to glance down at

his watch. Yes, he'd said he had to be somewhere, hadn't he? Pity. Apart from the danger, she would have enjoyed being here on her own with Matt. Silly. She gave herself a mental kick. Here they were, in a decidedly iffy situation and all she could think about was the way Matt had kissed her.

Matt touched her shoulder. 'They've gone,' he whispered. 'But I think we should give them a minute or two to get clear.'

'Absolutely.' She didn't want to be bumping into them. 'What's that noise?' The hairs on the back of her neck prickled with fear. Already, somewhere below them, she could hear the ominous crackling sounds. They had to get out. Now.

Matt strode to the stairs. 'They've set the place alight. Quick, back through the cupboard.' It was much easier with the stolen goods cleared out of the way. But on their own side, the smell was even stronger.

She could see the puddles of the

flammable liquid spreading over the floorboards, gleaming ominously. The petrol must have been set alight down in the jeweller's shop and so wouldn't catch up here for precious minutes. They had only to step across the oily patches to the door and they would be safe.

It all happened at once. Matt's mobile phone rang and a ball of flame leapt up into the room. Even as Sara was trying to register what was happening, Matt was pushing her back into their kitchen and slamming the door behind them. Sara sniffed, trying to work out whether there was any petrol in here but the smell seemed to have invaded her nose and she couldn't tell. 'Don't think so,' Matt said, as if she'd spoken aloud. 'But we haven't got much time.'

8

Sara glanced around the room. 'The skylight?' Matt was already climbing up on to the grubby draining board. 'Have you ever had it open? Doesn't matter. I'll break the rest of the glass if I have to.'

There was an old towel on a hook. Sara grabbed it and pushed it against the gap at the bottom of the door. Smoke. That's what you had to worry about most.

'Nearly there.' Matt was shoving at the skylight frame. 'Can you push at this side?'

Sara clambered up beside him, knowing that breaking the glass had to be a last resort. In this tiny room, they would be showered with lethal shards. She braced her hands against the wood.

'Together,' Matt said. 'Now!'

The frame groaned and burst open.

Cold clean air swept through the gap and behind them the fire roared at the door. She could feel the warmth from the old dry wooden panels. Already, without speaking, Matt was giving her a leg up on to the sill and she was out on to the roof, breathing deeply. He joined her, panting with the effort.

'We can't stay here.' They had only just made it. Wisps of deadly smoke were already seeping into the kitchen below.

'No.' He grinned at her. But their refuge was steep and slippery and the slates would soon become too warm for comfort. 'Up and away, I think. Lucky the shops are all joined together. Can you manage the roofs?'

She nodded. 'Yes, I'm fine.' She wasn't, but saying so would hardly be helpful. Besides, what choice did they have? At least there were gables and corners joining at odd angles wherever she looked which would be easier to hold on to.

Far below them, someone was

shouting. 'Hang on. I've dialled 999.' Sara peered down into the square. It was John. Thank goodness for that. He must have come back to check on his dubious employees but he could have had no idea what awaited him.

Matt waved in acknowledgement. 'That's good,' he muttered to Sara. 'We can wait if you like. Looks like there may be no need to risk our necks.'

Sara shook her head. 'The nearest fire station is miles away. I'll go for the neck risking option, thanks.' She hoped her voice was coming out as more than a squeak. She peered downwards again and saw Celia was there too. And now she recognised one or two others from the shops.

'They're looking for a ladder,' Matt was saying. 'If we can edge our way along past those chimneys to the end, they could reach us there.'

'OK.' They would be away from the heart of the fire anyway. A better position for waiting.

'I'll go first.' Matt lowered himself on

to the slates, spread-eagled so that he could gain maximum finger and toe-holds. 'You can rest your feet in the guttering.'

'I shouldn't rely on that too much.' As she spoke, a section fell away and there were screams from below. Sara hoped it hadn't fallen on the ladder party. She took a breath. Better get on with it, guttering or not. She held on to the sill and lowered herself to lie flat on the roof slates.

Matt reached out and grasped her hand and in spite of everything, she felt safer. As if a current of energy from Matt was spreading through her arms and legs, giving her strength, they slid along, a foot at a time.

Mark stopped, his arm round her waist. 'That's as far as we can go.'

They must have reached the end of the row. Here was the narrow passage leaving the square by Kevin's shop. Matt's face was close to hers. 'Hang on. It won't be long now.' Below them came a welcome clattering that had to be the promised ladder. 'It's OK. We're safe.'

'Yes.'

Long moments of nothing. How long could anyone take to set a ladder up? Matt squeezed her arm, reassuringly, but she couldn't feel reassured. Something was wrong. And then John's voice, several feet below them. 'This is the only one we could find and it's too short. But drop down to it and I'll catch you.'

So the ordeal was far from over. Sara risked a look down. John was at the top of the ladder, reaching upwards. But even if Matt held on to her and lowered her down, there would be a gap she didn't want to think about. And what about Matt? How would they both fit on to the ladder once John had caught her? She looked into Matt's eyes. 'I'm not leaving you up here.'

'Don't worry about me. And I won't let you down. Trust me.'

She knew that she did. She would trust this man with her life and was about to do just that. 'I do.'

'OK, then. I've got a grip on this drainpipe here. I can wedge my legs round the top as well. So I can lean forward until John catches you.'

She nodded, unable to rely on her voice. Every instinct was screaming that she couldn't do this. But what choice did she have? Already the slates, even here, were beginning to seem too warm for comfort. Within the ancient timbers of the roof spaces, the fire had enjoyed a free passage. Sara resolved she could not use Matt's strength one moment more than necessary — because whatever he said, if he leaned that little bit too far, he would be putting himself in grave danger.

Her legs left the security of the roof and her feet were dangling as she tried to get a sense of where the wall was. She was searching fruitlessly for a grip. 'It's all right,' John shouted. 'You can let go, Matt. I've got her.'

'Sure?'

'Yes.'

And suddenly Sara knew. In a moment she understood everything. All the little hints and signs she'd missed came together in a burst of illumination. John had known what was going on all the time. He had been directing his nephew and the others all along.

Had he ever been a true friend of hers or had the friendship merely suited his criminal purposes? Whatever the truth, she knew that she dared not trust him. She twisted her head to look down into John's face. He was smiling as she coaxed her. 'Come on. It's no distance at all.'

He also knew. There was no doubt about it. There was a ruthless contempt in the dark eyes that she had never noticed before. She wanted to shout 'No' but her voice had frozen in her throat.

She sensed a rush of movement below her and John was no longer there. The ladder was swaying. John was well out of reach as he leaped down to safety and the ladder fell. Matt swore.

She didn't know whether the scream came from herself or the group of spectators. All she knew was that her arms were being pulled from their sockets. 'I've got you,' Matt said. 'We're OK.'

She wanted to laugh. OK? She'd never been less OK. She heard herself asking, 'Is John all right?' Although she knew the answer already.

'Oh, yes,' Matt said. 'Don't worry about him. Now if you can move your left foot sideways, there's a spout jutting out. It should take some of your weight.'

She waggled her foot wildly, hardly noticing as she scraped her knee on the stone. Where was the dratted thing? Because now they were asking far too much of that drainpipe Matt was anchored against. At last something sharp jutted into her ankle.

'Now your right leg to the right. There's a bit of a ledge at the top of the signboard.' Matt's voice was calm. You would think he had all the time in the world instead of risking his life to save hers.

'I've got it.' She could hear the drainpipe creaking.

'That's good.'

John's voice came from below. 'Well done. I'm setting the ladder up again. Wait there, Sara, I'll get you.'

'Ignore him,' Matt muttered. 'If I heave, can you get your right knee up on to the gutter?'

'Yes.' Don't even think about whether the guttering would stand it. It had to. Her face was within an inch of Matt's now as he lay stretched downwards towards her. She could see the sweat on his forehead. 'Now.' And she was there, back up on the slates beside him.

Matt's arms were holding her tightly. 'I thought I'd lost you. That was deliberate. So no way are we going anywhere near that maniac's ladder.'

She said, before Mark could suggest it, 'We'll have to get over the gap.' They were overlooking the alley where the lovers' casements faced each other.

Don't think about what had happened there. It was only one of Kevin's tales. It shouldn't be too bad, surely? The passageway had always seemed so dark and narrow. From ground level, the upper storeys always seemed to lean together so quaintly.

She risked a glance. As she'd thought, up here the gap seemed horrendously wide. No way that the medieval lovers could have held hands, unless they'd had very long arms. And their eventual misadventure seemed all too probable.

Whatever she and Matt chose to do, they'd better get on with it. She looked down and over her shoulder to where John was again advancing up the ladder. He was still smiling. A sob caught in her throat. Who else was down there? Didn't they realise what he was trying to do? But no doubt from the ground, the failed attempt had appeared to be an unfortunate accident.

'If you hang on to me and I rest my

foot on that bracket that's holding the drainpipe,' Matt said, 'I can stride across to that small window ledge.'

'The lovers' casement.' Sara was trying to stop her teeth chattering.

'Whatever. If I kick the glass in, I can anchor myself inside and help you over.'

No time to argue. Already John was attempting to re-position the ladder in the passageway, shouting encouragement. More for the benefit of the group surrounding him than because he meant it. Except that she couldn't tell who the others were — if they were the group from the white van, she and Matt had no chance.

'Let's do it.' Would Matt be tall enough to stride it? He had to be. She moved one hand backwards a little and the slates immediately behind her were hot. Almost too hot to touch. Inside the roof-space, the upper floors of the whole row had become an inferno.

She leaned forward, hanging on to Matt's arm. And he launched himself out. Dimly she heard a gasp from below. Matt's foot almost slipped. There was the sound of breaking glass as his boot connected with the window. 'I've done it.' She let go at just the right time as his leg shot through the window, and he was holding on to the frame, his weight safely distributed on the other side of the gap. 'Wait there,' he called.

What else did he expect? She felt hysterical laughter welling within her chest. She looked down at the square and hardly made sense of what she was seeing. Running, shouting figures at the far end, immersed in some drama of their own. She didn't care because now she had to get over the gap herself. Matt reappeared, opening the window. 'It's OK. There's an old clothesline or something in here. And there's a hook for the line next to you. If I throw it over, you can secure it to that.'

'It won't take my weight.' She knew she wouldn't be able to make that stride without help. But she couldn't let Matt down, not after his heroic efforts.

'It won't have to. I'll take your weight, this will just steady you a bit. Giving you the confidence to make that first leap.'

He was right. She caught the end of the line and made it fast. In the open window, Matt was leaning out to her with his arms stretched wide. Suddenly she heard voices in the room beyond him. Not John! Her heart seemed to stop. Quickly she grasped the taut line with her right hand and strode out and down into space.

All over. Matt's arms were around her — and other faces and voices, concerned for her, asking if she was all right. And of course she was because now she recognised Kevin and Mr Carter from the bakery and one or two others. All genuinely friendly faces from the square. And it couldn't have been John, could it?

Because John had been at the centre of the mini-drama that had imprinted itself in her mind, she had seen him dropping the ladder and running across the square towards an agitated Celia. Celia's son was still there too, his shoulders hunched in defiance.

There was something wrong here. Something more than what had happened already. 'Let's get downstairs.'

'I've phoned for an ambulance as well as the fire brigade,' Kevin was saying. Somebody — probably Kevin, bless him, was trying to press them to come downstairs and sit down, pointing out to Matt that his leg was bleeding where he had kicked the window through. 'I'm fine,' Matt said. 'It's nothing. Just a few scratches.'

Sara said urgently, 'John's running away. I saw him running.'

'Oh, is he? Don't worry, I'll get him.' Matt was out on the cobbles, with Sara hurrying after him. 'After what he did to you? You realise he tried to kill you? Both of us?'

'I know. But leave it to the police.' She didn't want anything else to go wrong. And now there was no sign of

John. The youth in the dark baseball cap was running off in the opposite direction. There was only Celia, screaming in panic and wringing her hands, pointing to the craft shop. 'He's gone in there! Help him, please. Somebody help.'

The fire was raging along the upper floors but the glow downstairs seemed less fierce. Of course, on the ground floors, there had only been petrol in John's shop and the lower floors were separated by thick stone walls. The whole roof operation and escape must have taken only ten or twenty minutes although Sara felt as if time had stopped — and now smoke was billowing behind the adjoining shop windows.

'I'll get him,' Matt said. He turned to Celia. 'Why did he go in? What's he looking for? Is there somebody still alive in there?'

'The chair,' Celia moaned. 'He's gone to the chair. That's why I didn't come to collect it. I knew it would be safer in your shop. All those police searches . . . '

'In the corner beyond the cash till. At the back,' Sara said. 'Matt, you need some rope.' She didn't know whether he had heard her, he was pushing his sweater up over his nose and mouth. But Kevin had heard and was proffering what looked like another clothesline. 'I'll tie this round your waist,' Sara shouted. Matt was hardly waiting for her to finish the knot but it held as he ran in, and now she could see the glow of the first flames inside.

Sara's heart was squeezed in fear and yet part of her mind was wondering why John was risking his life for an old chair. And she did not want Matt to go in there but knew that he had to. Time seemed to be running in slow motion. 'Get down,' she said urgently, taking a tight hold of the other end of the line. 'Keep as near the floor as you can.' She wasn't even sure that Matt had heard. He bent double and was under the billowing smoke and lost to view.

Sara was muttering, 'Oh, Matt. Keep safe. Please. Please. Please.'

Matt peered through the billowing smoke. He could hear Sara's voice in his head, with the direction clear and calm. He knew exactly where to go — and there was the chair, smouldering but not yet ablaze. He pulled his sweater over his mouth, trying not to breathe. Where was John?

The figure rose from the chair itself, coughing and spluttering and on the point of collapse, his hand to his chest. Matt resisted the temptation to call out. Wouldn't help either of them if he filled his lungs with smoke.

John saw him at last and seemed to be pushing him away, the fool. Stupid to come in here in the first place, Matt wasn't expecting any assistance from him.

He grasped John's arms, twisted him round to get him in a lock and dragged him towards the door. He could hardly see it now. Thank goodness for Sara's clothesline. At least John was no longer resisting. They would make it. They had to, because Sara was out there waiting for them.

Other people were gathering round her as they saw what was happening at this end of the square. 'Help me,' she cried to Celia who was still weeping uselessly. 'Be ready to pull.' But Kevin was by her side. 'It's all right. I've got it.'

It would have meant a blessed relief for her aching arms, but Sara was determined to hang on. The rope was suddenly taut — and then slack as if there was a dead weight at the other end. 'Please no,' Sara cried out. Not that. After what seemed an hour, while her heart thumped and her wrists felt as if they would snap, at last the rope responded within her hands, as if someone inside was taking the weight in return and moving towards her.

As if Matt had struggled to his feet. He'd done it. He had to be OK. He just had to be. She peered into the smoke but she could imagine what was happening so clearly, it was as if she could see.

Two figures, at last, Matt supporting the other and with a roar, the shop itself burst into full and vibrant flame behind them. She ran to hold him up and to help, half closing her eyes against the heat. Others were taking John from him and lowering him to the round.

Sara hardly noticed. She was clinging to Matt, feeling the strength of his arms around her as the sirens of the fire engine and ambulance blared behind them.

9

Celia was screaming as her arms flailed in anguish. 'John, John. Is it all right? Please tell me. Let me through, I'm his sister.' Regardless of what her brother had just been through, she was shaking his arm.

Sara was only just taking in what Celia had said. 'Celia, please. He's badly burned.' Was what all right? What did Celia mean?

John opened his eyes. 'I got it.' He hardly seemed to know where he was or who was witnessing this declaration. Or that Matt was standing right next to him. Sara's eyes were drawn to John's hand, which was clasped to his chest half hiding something that danced and flickered, reflecting the light of the flames. Sara gasped. There was no mistaking it. John was holding the Allenwick Star.

Celia was still shouting into John's face. 'Is it in your pocket?'

Swiftly but gently, not wanting to cause further pain, Sara prised the jewel from John's fingers as Celia at last realised what was happening. 'No,' Celia screeched, grabbing Sara's arm and with a murderous look in her eyes. 'You can't. Not after everything we've been through to get it. I hid it in the chair when the police were sniffing around. How did I know those fools would set the place on fire?'

'It's not yours and you know it.' Sara said. 'This belongs to Helen Allenwick.'

Celia raised her hand and the flames glinted on the small craft knife she held. But Matt was behind her, clutching her arm and the knife fell to the ground. Celia turned to run and they all saw that a police car was rounding the corner of the square. 'It's finished, Celia,' Sara said quietly. Celia sank down on to her knees on the cobbles, weeping with rage and frustration.

John's eyes were closed. Even the

howling of the approaching emergency vehicles brought no response. Sara knelt down and tried to find a pulse in his neck and thank goodness, there were signs of life. She looked round frantically. Where was the ambulance? Matt was on his knees beside her, panting. He must have treatment too, Sara thought urgently. Smoke inhalation.

'Sara.' It was John's voice, hoarse and almost unrecognisable. 'Need to speak — to the nephew.' His eyes flickered open. 'He saved me.'

She turned in surprise. 'Yes, of course. Matt's here. Right next to you.'

'I hear you,' Matt croaked.

'Tell your uncle — I'll say he didn't do it.'

'It's all right,' Matt said. 'Don't try to speak. The paramedics are here.'

'No, I must. Might not have another chance.' John grasped Sara's arm and his grip was surprisingly strong. 'I did it. I killed Frank Chesters. Forty years ago. Robbery. We both needed the money, Paul Peasholm and I.

'Both on the verge of bankruptcy. But it was my idea. I talked him into it. Knew Frank left cash in his shop overnight. But we didn't know he would be there. Not so late. I panicked. I had a knife with me. And then I told Paul it would be my word against his and he'd be the one to take the most blame. Because he was so much older than me.'

'Yes,' Matt said. 'I'll tell him.' He and Sara looked at each other. Both with the same thought. 'That's why you were able to use the rooms over our shop to store stolen goods.'

Sara said, 'You were blackmailing him.' Poor Mr P, she thought, carrying such a burden all this time. He had been present at a terrible crime and must obviously take some of the blame. But better if he had owned up to his part in it straightaway. His debt to society would have been paid years ago.

But John, the once-trusted friend who had deceived her so cleverly, had again lapsed into unconsciousness.

'Amazing,' Sara said happily, 'how everyone has pulled together on this.' it was a year later and the square was crowded with cheerful, enthusiastic people. All there to attend the official opening of the new Phoenix craft centre and workshops which now filled the side of the square where the fire had taken place.

The original shop fronts had been lovingly restored under Matt's direction. He had put all of his skills and energy into making this project work, with Sara backing him all the way.

She waved to where Mr P was sitting beside Helen. His trial was at last behind him and having regard to his age and infirmity, he had received a suspended sentence. But John had recovered from his burns to begin his term in prison and Celia's son had also received his just deserts. Celia moved away several months ago. There was no way she would be appearing at today's event.

Someone said, 'This will put Beckthwaite on the tourist map,' and Sara laughed and nodded. Because if she had heard that once, she must have heard it a hundred times. But it was true.

Matt was crossing the square towards her and his eyes lit up as he caught sight of her in the throng. 'Ready?'

'Not quite.' She smiled at him. 'Just one thing first.'

'What's that?' She knew he would be mentally going through the list of all the ingredients that were making this day so special. Refreshments, speeches, curtain ready for the mayor to reveal the Phoenix plaque . . .

'Nothing to do with any of that,' Sara said. She put her hands around his neck and pulled his face down to hers. The sun glinted on the diamond in her engagement ring. The noise and the jostling, cheery crowd were completely forgotten as they kissed.

'Good luck, my love,' Sara whispered. Not that he needed luck. This new venture would work, she knew it would.

They would make it work together.

She would never regret the way she had learned to trust a stranger and follow her heart.

THE END

HER HEART'S DESIRE

Dorothy Taylor

When Beth Garland's great aunt Emily dies, she leaves Greg, her boyfriend, in Manchester — along with her successful advertising job — to return to live in Emily's cottage. Feeling disillusioned with Greg and his high-handed attitude, she finds herself more and more attracted to her aunt's gardener, Noah. But Noah seems to be hiding from the past, whilst Greg has his own ideas about the direction of their relationship. Surrounded by secrecy and deceit, how will Beth ever find true love?

PRECIOUS MOMENTS

June Gadsby

The heartbreak was all behind her, but hearing her name mentioned on the radio, and that song — their special song — brought bittersweet memories rushing back through the years. It had to be a coincidence, and was best forgotten — but then Lara opened the door to find her past standing there. The moment of truth she had dreaded for years had finally arrived, and she wasn't sure how to handle it . . .

THE SECRET OF SHEARWATER

Diney Delancey

When Zoe Carson inherits a cottage in Cornwall, she takes a holiday from her job in London to stay at the cottage. There, she makes friends with the local people, including the hot-tempered Gregory Enodoc. Zoe is glad of their friendship when events take a sinister turn and the police become involved. And when she decides to leave London to live permanently at the cottage, Zoe is unaware of the dangers into which this will lead her . . .

SWEET CHALLENGE

Joyce Johnson

London life for Chloe Duncan is changed forever when she accepts an invitation to visit her previously unknown Scottish great aunt, Flora Duncan. Chloe loves the peace and beauty of rural Highland life at Flora's croft, but mysteries and tensions in her great aunt's past disturb this tranquillity. Land disputes involve her in danger and, whilst unravelling the mystery of Flora's lost love, Chloe's own heart is jeopardised when she meets handsome New Zealander Steve McGlarran . . .